Claudia and Crazy Peaches

**Other books by
Ann M. Martin**

Rachel Parker, Kindergarten Show-off
Eleven Kids, One Summer
Ma and Pa Dracula
Yours Turly, Shirley
Ten Kids, No Pets
Slam Book
Just a Summer Romance
Missing Since Monday
With You and Without You
Me and Katie (the Pest)
Stage Fright
Inside Out
Bummer Summer

BABY-SITTERS LITTLE SISTER series
THE BABY-SITTERS CLUB mysteries
THE BABY-SITTERS CLUB series

Claudia and Crazy Peaches
Ann M. Martin

AN
APPLE
PAPERBACK

SCHOLASTIC INC.
New York Toronto London Auckland Sydney

Cover art by Hodges Soileau

No part of this publication may be reproduced in whole or in part, or stored in a retrieval system, or transmitted in any form or by any means, electronic, mechanical, photocopying, recording, or otherwise, without written permission of the publisher. For information regarding permission, write to Scholastic Inc., 555 Broadway, New York, NY 10012.

ISBN 0-590-48222-X

12 11 10 9 8 7 6 5 4 3   4 5 6 7 8 9/9

Printed in the U.S.A.

First Scholastic printing, September 1994

The author gratefully acknowledges
Jahnna Beecham and Malcolm Hillgartner
for their help in
preparing this manuscript.

CHAPTER 1

Have you ever had one of those tingly feelings — the kind that tells you something is going to happen, but you're not sure what or where or when? That's the feeling I had when I opened my eyes on Monday morning.

"Claudia!" Mom called from downstairs. "Are you up?"

"I'm up," I mumbled, not moving.

"Better hurry. You don't want to be late for school."

Want to bet?

I lay on my back staring at the ceiling, where I had painted little stars and moons the week before. As an artist, I have this theory: if you can't eat it or wear it — paint it. That's what helped me decide to use the walls and ceiling of my room as my canvas. I also paint clothes (I tie-dye them, too) and shoes. I have several pairs of high-top sneakers that I decorated in glitter and puff paint. I even have a pair of ballet flats that are entirely covered in red sequins. I call them my ruby slippers, after Dorothy's in *The Wizard of Oz*.

Anyway, I was staring at the purple polka dot cow I'd painted jumping over a silver moon, and I got that tingly feeling again. It was definitely not my usual Monday morning feeling.

I'm generally grumpy at the start of the week. I think most kids feel pretty cranky on Monday mornings, except those few mutant types who leap out of bed at the crack of dawn and can't wait to hurry to school and take a test so they can add yet another A to their straight A record. (Have you guessed that I'm not exactly your model student?)

School is okay. There are even one or two classes I really enjoy, like art. But there are some classes, like English — particularly spelling — that practically paralyze me. I don't know why that is. Neither do my parents. They think I don't apply myself and that I need to study harder. They may be right. Let's face it, I don't spend every single night slaving over my homework. I have a well-rounded life, unlike my sister Janine, who's a junior in high school but also takes college classes. Can you believe it? No wonder my parents are disappointed in my grades. But it's really hard to compete with a total genius.

Anyway, back to my tingly feeling. What could possibly be causing it? Nothing special was scheduled at school. After school, I had my regular Monday Baby-sitters Club meeting. Hmm. I wondered if that was it. Kristy Thomas (our club president) had talked the week before about wanting to start a fall project. Along with the baby-sitting, the Baby-sitters Club organizes lots of fun activities, like neighborhood carnivals and talent shows. Once we even had an ecology fair and got our whole school involved in recycling and conservation. But maybe I should tell you more about myself, and then fill you in on the Baby-sitters Club.

My full name is Claudia Lynn Kishi, but sometimes my friends call me Claud. I'm thirteen and I'm in eighth grade at Stoneybrook Middle School. I have dark, almond-shaped eyes and long, jet black hair. (My family is Japanese-American.) I love to read mysteries, Nancy Drew being my absolute fave. And I'm crazy about junk food. Doritos, Mallomars, Ring Dings — you name it and I'll eat it. You'd think I'd have a pretty bad complexion from all of those sweets, but by some miracle, my skin is clear (which drives my friends crazy!).

I also love clothes. Dressing is like another art form for me. I really enjoy putting unusual combinations together. I'll wear suspenders backwards with tuxedo pants and a long sleeved T-shirt that I've tie-dyed myself. Or I'll cover an entire jean vest with tiny safety pins and funky plastic charms from a gumball machine and wear that with a jean skirt and bright red cowboy boots.

"Claudia, you have exactly five minutes to get dressed and eat breakfast," Mom called from downstairs. "Make that four and a half minutes." Can you tell my mother is a stickler for detail? She is head librarian at the Stoneybrook Library, and she likes for things to be accurate.

"I'll be right down," I called as I switched into high gear. Mondays are hard enough as it is. But being late for school on a Monday is the worst, because the teachers are feeling just as grumpy as the students. I had no time to think about my wardrobe. I just made it up as I went along. I slipped on a pair of baggy jeans with an extra long belt and grabbed a pinstriped vest to go over my white shirt. For color, I wore my purple high-tops and a black derby with a pink-and-purple hatband.

"Two minutes and counting." Mom handed me a piece of toast covered in peanut butter and half an apple as I passed her in the hall. "That should hold you until lunchtime."

"Thanks, Mom." I gave her a quick hug. "I'll see you after school."

"Be sure to come straight home," Mom called from the front steps. (It's a habit of hers — shouting last minute instructions to me as I go down the block.) "You'll be receiving a very important phone call around four o'clock."

"Phone call?" I screeched to a halt (as much as you can screech in sneakers). "From who?"

"Peaches. She called with some big news while you were still asleep."

Peaches just happens to be one of my favorite people on the planet. She's also my mom's sister, but you'd never know it to meet her. While Mom is organized and, well, mom-like, Peaches is carefree and fun, which is more kidlike. A phone call from her is always a big thrill.

"What news?" I ran back to Mom and hopped up and down in front of her. "Tell me! Tell me!"

Mom ran her hand across her mouth. "My lips are sealed. Peaches wants to tell you herself."

"But I can't wait a whole day to talk to her. I'll die of agony. Couldn't you just give me a little hint?"

Mom grinned but shook her head firmly.

"Nope. Not even one." She checked her watch. "Now hurry, or you really will be late for school."

I would have stayed longer, pleading for just a little clue, but I spied my best friend, Stacey McGill, standing at the end of my walk, making last minute adjustments to her hair.

"Pick up the pace, Claud," Stacey called. "I'm supposed to meet Robert on the front steps *before* school."

"I'm coming. I'm coming."

What was with everybody today? It seemed as if they were all moving in fast motion and I was slogging through Jell-O trying to keep up.

"Mary Anne and Mal said they couldn't wait any longer, so they went on ahead," Stacey said as I fell in step beside her. "I think Mary Anne needed to see Logan before school and Mal wanted to talk to Jessi about a report they were doing together."

Like me, Stacey, Mary Anne, Mallory, Logan, and Jessi are all members of the Baby-sitters Club. They live in my neighborhood, and most days we walk to school together. It's nice having a big group of friends, but I also like spending time just with Stacey.

"Don't tell anyone," I whispered, looping my arm through Stacey's. "But I'm glad it's just you and me today."

Stacey grinned. "Me too. I feel as though I hardly see you anymore."

"Especially now that you and Robert are together," I teased. Robert Brewster is Stacey's new boyfriend. He's totally great looking, and just as nice as he is gorgeous.

"And especially since you've become the professional matchmaker of SMS."

Stacey was referring to this column I write for the SMS newspaper. It was something I'd originally started in hopes of meeting the perfect boy. Mr. Wonderful never came along, but I continued with the column. I really enjoy putting people together.

Stacey and I shuffled through the red and gold leaves that had fallen from the sycamore trees lining Bradford Court. As we headed for school, we caught each other up on the latest events in our lives. I told her about my new art project.

"I'm working on a sculpture made entirely of non-biodegradable material. Like Styrofoam cups and plates and plastic bottles and — "

"How about disposable diapers?" Stacey asked.

"Ew!" I squealed. "Everything but that."

"Does your sculpture have a title?"

I nodded. "I came up with the perfect name. I'm calling it 'Forever Yours.' "

"That is perfect."

Then it was Stacey's turn to talk. Most of what she had to say was about Robert, and what a fun time they'd had that weekend. Before I knew it we'd reached the front steps of SMS, the bell had rung, and another fun-filled day of school had begun. I didn't even get a chance to tell Stacey about my phone call from Peaches. I figured I'd wait to tell her after I heard the big news.

The day passed at a snail's pace. I barely squeaked by with a C on a pop quiz in math class, which, as usual, was totally confusing. Science was actually kind of fun. We had to draw pictures of the stomach and all the parts that attach to it. After lunch I could barely concentrate on the rest of my classes. I just kept thinking about Peaches and my upcoming phone call.

You probably think Peaches is a weird name for a Japanese-American to have. Well, it's not what my grandmother named her. Her real name is Miyoshi. (My mom's name is Rioko.) Her husband, Russ, called her Peaches and it just sort of stuck. Russ isn't Japanese. He's "American-American" (actually, I think his grandparents came from Ireland) and has red hair, freckles, and a big friendly grin. Anyway, I've always known Peaches as Peaches, and I've always been crazy about her — and Russ. They lived in Stoneybrook until I was about seven. They used to take Janine and me to the park all the time. Russ and I would climb trees while Peaches would hang from the monkey bars (Janine would just watch and smile).

Once, when we'd had a really terrible storm, Russ wanted to check on us to see if we were okay. He'd broken his ankle and couldn't walk, and the storm had blown down so many trees that the roads were closed, so he couldn't drive, either. But Russ found a way — he rode over in a golf cart!

As I thought about all of my Peaches and Russ adventures, I realized that one of the last times I'd seen them had been a very sad occasion.

That was at Mimi's funeral. Mimi was my grandmother and my very special friend. She understood me better than anyone else. Whenever I was upset or confused, Mimi was there to comfort me. Sometimes she'd make a cup of her special tea and sit next to me while I drank it. Other times she'd just stroke my hair and murmur, "My Claudia." I always felt better, just knowing she was there and that she cared. It's weird, but sometimes I'll forget she's gone and run into her room to tell her some little bit of news or to show her some new piece of art that I'm proud of. Then I remember, and a knot forms in my chest and my eyes fill with tears. It's still hard to accept that someone I loved so much could be gone.

Mimi's death hit everyone hard. Even Peaches, who is usually so bright and cheery, found it difficult to put on a happy face for months afterward. I think part of that had to do with the fact that she and Russ had never given Mimi grandchildren. I knew that they both wanted kids badly — but they were both serious about their careers, too.

Brrrring!

I sat up with a start, trying to remember where I was. I blinked several times and realized I was in Mrs. Hall's English class. Everyone around me was gathering their books and heading for the door.

"Now remember, class," Mrs. Hall called, "I'll need those reports back by tomorrow. It shouldn't be too hard if you've read the chapter and paid attention in class."

What reports? I wanted to shout. I hadn't heard her mention any reports. I hadn't heard her say anything. Then I realized I'd spent the entire class daydreaming. Now I was going to have to go home, read my chapter, call somebody to tell me what I'd missed in class, *and* write a report. It was going to be a long night.

That afternoon, I think I brought home work from every class in school, including art. My "Forever Yours" sculpture was due in less than two weeks and I knew I'd need to work on it outside of school to get it just right. Still, I didn't sit down to work the instant I reached my house. I walked in my front door, dropped my (enormous) stack of books, and fixed myself a snack of graham crackers smothered in peanut butter and topped with (my favorite) chocolate chips. Yum!

I scarfed that down and was about to fix myself another plateful when the phone rang. I checked the clock. Four already? (Wow, time sure flies when you're eating chocolate.)

"That's for me!" I bellowed up the stairs to no one in particular. If I'd thought about it I would have remembered that I was the only one home. Mom and Dad were still at work and Janine was at one of her college classes. Anyway, I dove for the phone, anxious to talk to my aunt.

"Hello, Peaches?" I shouted into the phone. "Is that you?"

"Of course, it's me," Peaches replied. "Is that you?"

"Tell me your news," I cried. "I can't stand it another second."

"Okay, but first I want you to make sure you put me and Russ on your Baby-sitters Club client list."

"But our client list is for people with — " I never finished my sentence. I let out a loud whoop of delight.

"I've just gone deaf," Peaches cracked. "Was that a siren or a shriek?"

"Oh, Peaches!" I gushed. "Are you really going to have a baby?"

"That's what the doctor tells me. In about seven months."

"I'm so happy for you." I couldn't help it. Suddenly my eyes were brimming with tears and my voice had gone completely shaky. "Tell Russ congratulations."

"Thanks, honey," Peaches said, sounding a little shaky herself. "We've waited a long time for this baby. I'm ecstatic."

"Oh," I suddenly gasped. "That means I'm going to have a new cousin."

"That's right," Peaches said. "And I expect you to teach your new cousin all the important things in life, like how to climb trees — "

"And hang by your knees from the monkey bars," I added with a giggle.

"But first she has to learn to walk," Peaches reminded me.

"She?" I repeated. "Are you hoping for a girl?"

"I don't care if it's a girl or a boy," Peaches declared. "Just so long as she, or he, is healthy."

We talked for a few more minutes, then Peaches had to run. She was trying a new recipe for an all-vegetable casserole from the

12

Eating Right for Pregnant Women cookbook. The timer on her oven had just signaled it was done.

The second I hung up I started dancing around the kitchen and nearly crashed into the table. So that's what my tingly feeling had been about! Wonderful Peaches and Russ were going to have a baby. At last!

I couldn't wait to break the news to my friends. Luckily for me, the Baby-sitters Club meeting was at five-thirty, so I didn't have long to wait.

CHAPTER 2

"Rock-a-bye baby on the tree top," I sang as I vacuumed my room. "When the wind blows, the cradle will — "

"I don't believe it!" Kristy Thomas announced from the door to my room. "Call the newspapers. Claudia Kishi is cleaning her room *and* singing lullabies. She must have lost her mind."

"Very funny." I clicked off the vacuum cleaner. "I just happen to be turning over a new leaf."

"What leaf?" Mary Anne Spier peered over Kristy's shoulder. "If you want leaves, our front yard is covered with them. It's going to take a week to rake them all up."

Kristy turned to Mary Anne and explained, with a very serious face, "Claudia's not collecting leaves, she's turning them over."

"Turning over leaves?" Stacey called from behind them as she came up the stairs.

"What's that, some kind of performance art?"

Can you tell that Baby-sitters Club meetings can get awfully silly? Of course, they can also be pretty serious, but today was definitely a goofy day.

Before I tell you any more about the meeting, I should keep my promise to tell you about the club and everyone in it. Here goes.

The Baby-sitters Club history has to start with Kristy Thomas, our president. It was Kristy's great idea to form the club and it's Kristy's even greater ideas that keep it running smoothly. Her own story is a little complicated. You see, she used to live right across the street from me with her mom, who was divorced, and her three brothers, Charlie (who is seventeen, and in high school), Sam (he's fifteen) and David Michael (age seven). Then Kristy's mom fell in love with this millionaire named Watson Brewer and everybody's lives changed. First, Mrs. Thomas married Watson and became Mrs. Brewer. Then the whole Thomas family moved from their nice little house on Bradford Court to Watson's huge mansion across town. It's a good thing he has a mansion, because ten people live there most of the time. How'd they end up with ten? Well, you see, Watson has two kids of his own: Karen, who's seven, and Andrew, who's four. They live with Watson every other month. After Watson and Kristy's mom got married, they adopted Emily Michelle from Vietnam, who is two and a half. Then Nannie, Kristy's grandmother, moved in to help look after Emily, and that brought the total to ten.

What else can I say about Kristy? She has brown hair and brown eyes. She's the shortest girl in the eighth grade, but she more than makes up for it with her big personality. Kristy's a natural leader. Besides being president of our club, she coaches Kristy's Krushers, a neighborhood softball team. Kristy's a real athlete and dresses like one. No frills — just jeans, a turtleneck, a sweater, and sneakers. It's practically her uniform. Sometimes Kristy can be stubborn and bossy, but I guess that goes with being a leader. One other thing about Kristy — she won't admit it, but she has this semi-romance going with a guy named Bart Taylor. They're made for each other. Bart coaches a softball team called Bart's Bashers, he's crazy about Kristy, *and* they both like anchovies (ew! ick!). See? A perfect match.

I'm the BSC vice-president. Not because I have any presidential skills, but because I have my own phone and number. Pretty neat, huh? That's why we hold the meetings in my room. I do the artwork for our club fliers and share my snacks (which are generally stashed out of sight, under the bed or behind a box of art supplies, since my parents don't approve of my junk-food habit).

You already know all about me, so I'll move on to the treasurer of the BSC, my best friend, Anastasia Elizabeth McGill. If I had to come up with a list of words to describe Stacey, I'd write: smart, gorgeous, ultra-cool, and sophisticated. She looks and acts a lot older than she is, partly because she grew up in New York City and partly (I think) because of her diabetes. I don't mean that diabetes ages you or anything like that. In case you don't know (and I didn't until I met Stacey), diabetes is a disease that keeps your body from processing sugar properly. So Stacey has to stay on a strict diet and never, ever break it. She also has to give herself shots (ew!) of insulin every single day. It's more responsibility than the average thirteen-year-old has to deal with, and that's why I think it's made her more mature. Stacey's learned to live with being a diabetic, so it's not a big deal, except for those times when there's extra pressure in her life and she forgets to take care of herself. Then it can be scary. Stacey has even had to go into the hospital since I've known her.

Of all of us, I'd have to say that Stacey has had the most crushes on guys in her life. There was Toby (he gave Stacey her first kiss, in the

Tunnel of Luv at Sea City) and Pete Black, and Pierre, and Terry, and Wes, her math student-teacher. She was even seeing Kristy's older brother Sam for awhile. But ever since she met Robert Brewster she hasn't given other guys a thought. Robert used to be a big basketball star at SMS, but he quit the team when he thought the school was putting too much emphasis on sports. Isn't that cool?

One more thing about Stacey. She's a real math whiz, which is why she's the BSC's treasurer. Stacey keeps track of the club dues, doles out the money we have to spend (to help pay my phone bill, for example), and occasionally lets us know when there's a little extra money left over, for fun stuff like slumber parties with pizza and ice cream.

Next comes Mary Anne Spier, the secretary of the BSC. Mary Anne is best friends with Kristy, but they are as different as night and day. While Kristy is really outgoing and forceful, Mary Anne is shy and sweet. She is also emotional. (I think I'd have to underline the word *emotional*.) Mary Anne cries over cute kittens, sad movies, and I've even seen her cry at TV commercials.

We elected Mary Anne secretary because she has the best handwriting. But, fortunately for the BSC, she's also very conscientious and organized. She'd have to be to handle everything she does for us.

You see, here's how our club works: we meet at my house Monday, Wednesday, and Friday afternoons, from five-thirty to six. Parents can call us at those times to arrange sitters. Currently, there are seven of us (plus one associate — don't worry, I'll explain in a minute) so they're practically guaranteed a sitter. Mary Anne keeps a record book with all of our schedules in it, listing not just our sitting jobs but our after school activities, too, such as Kristy's Krushers practices and my art classes. When a client calls, Mary Anne checks the book to see who's available, and then, after we've decided who'll take the job, we call the client back, and Mary Anne writes the new job down. And (are you ready for this?) Mary Anne has never made a mistake.

Until a year or two ago, Mary Anne led a pretty sheltered life. Her mom died when Mary Anne was just a baby, and her dad raised her all by himself. He was very strict. Mary Anne couldn't go anywhere after school, she wasn't allowed to talk on the phone (unless it was about homework), and, worst of all, she had to dress in really babyish clothes. I'm not kidding. Her dad made her wear these old-fashioned dresses with knee socks, and she had to keep her hair in braids. But fortunately, things have changed. Mary Anne has grown up some, and her dad has loosened up some. Now Mary Anne can wear what she wants, and she's cut her hair. She even has a boyfriend, Logan Bruno.

Besides being cute (Mary Anne thinks Logan looks just like the star Cam Geary), funny, and charming (he's got this really great Southern drawl), Logan is also an associate member of the BSC. (Remember, I said I'd explain that.) This means he doesn't usually come to meetings, but he helps us out if we get really busy and need extra sitters.

Early on, the BSC decided to have an alternate officer, so that someone would always be able to fill in when a regular officer is sick. Dawn Schafer is usually our alternate officer, but right now she's in California, spending some time with her dad and brother, Jeff.

Dawn has long, sun-bleached blonde hair, a great tan, and a real laid back style. She eats what I call rabbit food — lettuce, carrots, bean sprouts, all that healthy stuff. How did a California girl end up in Connecticut? Well, not too long ago, Dawn's parents divorced, and Dawn and her mom and brother moved to Stoneybrook, where Dawn's mom had grown up. Dawn met Mary Anne and they instantly became best friends. Shortly after that, the two of them were flipping through Mrs. Schafer's old high school yearbook and they discovered that Dawn's mom and Mary Anne's dad had once been in love. Amazing, huh? So Mary Anne and Dawn brought their parents together to see what would happen. Guess what? It was love at first sight all over again. Before too long Mr. Spier married Mrs. Shafer. Then Mary Anne and her dad moved into Dawn's house, which is this two hundred-year-old farmhouse with a barn and wonderful trees and, best of all, a secret passage. It leads from the barn right into Dawn's room. She thinks it might be haunted. (I hope so. Ghost stories are almost as good as mysteries!)

So there they were — Mary Anne and her dad, Dawn and her mom, and Mary Anne's kitten, Tigger, all living happily ever after in the farmhouse. Or at least that's what we all thought was happening. I mean, they were happy, but Dawn started really missing her father and Jeff (who had moved back with his dad a while earlier), and her old home and friends. It was a sad day for the Baby-sitters Club when Dawn broke the news that she was going back to California. Everybody understands, and we know Dawn will be back here before long, but we all really miss her. Mary Anne misses her most of all.

When Dawn went to California, Shannon

Kilbourne, who used to be an associate member (like Logan), moved into the role of alternate officer. Shannon lives in Kristy's new neighborhood. When they first met, Kristy called Shannon a snob, but she soon found out how open and friendly Shannon really is. Shannon and her two younger sisters, Tiffany and Maria, go to Stoneybrook Day School, a private school across town. Shannon's an excellent student. She's also really cute. She has thick, curly blonde hair and these piercing blue eyes.

And last, but definitely not least, are our two junior officers and the youngest members of the BSC, Mallory Pike and Jessica Ramsey. Mal and Jessi are best friends. They have lots in common; they're both in the sixth grade, each is the oldest kid in her family, they're both big readers, and they're crazy about horses. Those two go berserk over horse movies — I think they've watched *The Black Stallion* about a zillion times — and horse books. Name any horse book and I'll bet they've read it, especially if it's by Marguerite Henry.

But Mal and Jessi are hardly Tweedledum and Tweedledee. They're very different in some ways. Mal has eight, count 'em, eight kids in her family. Jessi has three. Mal wants to be a children's book writer and illustrator when she grows up, while Jessi is well on her way to becoming a ballerina. She's already danced the lead in several productions. And even if they dressed alike, they'd never be mistaken for twins — Mallory is white and Jessi is black. Of course, that doesn't make any difference to them, or to the rest of us, but believe it or not, when the Ramseys first moved to Stoneybrook, a few people were upset. Which is pretty disgusting and sad. But all that seems to be behind them now. These days the Ramseys are settled in and happy.

So that's the Baby-sitters Club. A great bunch of friends. And a great business.

Anyway, there I was, still holding the vacuum cleaner, when I heard another voice say, "Claudia, who are you trying to kid? I know that's not a real vacuum cleaner." It was Shannon. She was standing with Stacey, Kristy, and Mary Anne, peering into my room. Behind her, I could just see Mal and Jessi.

I flicked on the switch and aimed the hose at Shannon and the group. "One more crack like that and you're all history!"

Before anyone could respond, Kristy pointed at my digital clock. It was just turning from five twenty-nine to five-thirty. "Order. Put your weapon away, Claud. The BSC meeting has officially begun."

Just at that second the phone rang. Stacey made a dive for it while I switched off the vacuum. "Baby-sitters Club, this is Stacey."

We watched Stacey as she murmured, "Uh-huh. Uh-huh. Yes, that's right. How did you hear about us?" Pause. "Well, we're glad you called. Uh-huh, uh-huh. How old? That's fine. Let me talk to the others and I'll call you right back."

She put the phone on the hook and smiled. "We have a new client. That was Mrs. Springer. She has a seven-year-old daughter named Natalie."

Kristy snapped her fingers. "Wait a minute. I know that name. Natalie is a friend of Karen's."

"Well, Mrs. Springer needs a sitter for Thursday afternoon."

Mary Anne checked the book. "Jessi can't do it. I can't, Kristy can't. That leaves Shannon — "

"Oops, sorry," Shannon interrupted. "I have a special French club meeting that day. It was just announced this afternoon."

Mary Anne carefully penciled in Shannon's meeting. "That leaves Mal and Claudia."

"Claudia, would you mind taking it?" Mallory asked me. "I have to help my sister with her poetry this week."

I had just finished coiling up the vacuum cleaner cord and was rewarding myself with a bag of chocolate-covered peanuts. My mouth

24

was full, so all I could do was mumble a reply.

Jessi, who was sitting on the floor in front of Mary Anne, leaned back and said, "That sounded like 'Fur, I'll fake it,' but I think she meant to say 'Sure, I'll take it.' "

I laughed so hard that peanuts exploded out of my mouth.

"Ew! Total gross-out!" Stacey squealed, which made me laugh even harder.

I crossed my arms and gave Stacey my sternest face. "Look what you made me do. Now I'll have to vacuum all over again."

Of course this made everyone laugh. When the phone rang next, it was hard finding someone to answer it without breaking down and giggling. Luckily Kristy, our fearless leader, took that call.

There were five more calls before I was able to break the news about Peaches. I did it by taking the end of the vacuum cleaner tube and blowing into it like a trumpet.

"Ta-ta-ta-DA! May I have your attention, please. I have a very important announcement to make."

It was exactly six o'clock and my friends were in the process of gathering their things to leave. Everyone froze.

I was smiling so hard my face hurt but I tried to keep my voice calm so I could get out my news. "I just found out less than an hour ago that my favorite aunt and uncle in the whole world are going to have a baby."

Stacey, who knows and loves them almost as much as I do, gasped, "Peaches and Russ are having a baby?"

"Yes!" I shrieked. "At long last, I'm going to have a cousin!"

Suddenly the room exploded with cheers. It was a complete pile-on as everyone jumped on me. We fell backwards onto my bed in one big happy heap.

CHAPTER 3

"Why are you mashing your peas?" Mom asked me at dinner a couple of nights later.

"So they'll go with my mashed potatoes," I explained as I smashed my fork down on three big juicy ones. "I thought the dinner should have a theme."

"That's fine," Dad said, raising an eyebrow at me as I started to work on my meatloaf. "Just so long as you eat it after you smash it."

Let's face it — mashed potatoes, peas, and meatloaf ranks right up in the Top Ten of yucky dinners. Unfortunately, coordinating the meal didn't help. Now that my food was all on one level, the thought of eating it was even more repulsive. Luckily for me, I was saved by the bell. Or I should say, the ring.

"Now, who would be calling during dinner?" Mom grumbled as she scooted back her chair and stood up to answer the phone. "I'll tell whoever it is to call back."

But she didn't. Instead, my normally calm mother squealed (yes, squealed!), "Oh, Peaches, that's wonderful news!"

"What?" In a flash I was by Mom's side. "I want to know."

Mom cupped her hand over the mouthpiece. "Russ and Peaches are buying a new house. Their old one will be too small for them, so they're moving. To Stoneybrook!"

"Hooray!" Janine and I both shouted. Then I raced to get on the extension.

"When are you guys coming?" I cried.

"That's the hitch," Russ replied. "You see, we found a buyer for our house but we have to move out in about a week and a half. We can't move into our new house until a month later. We're hunting for a place to stay."

"Well, of course you'll stay with us," Mom said firmly.

"Are you sure?" Peaches asked. "I mean, six people is a houseful. And a month is an awfully long time."

"You're coming here," Mom insisted. "And that's that."

"Oh, Ri," Peaches gushed, "you are so wonderful."

"What will you do with your furniture?" I asked, imagining it all stacked up in our living room.

"We'll put that in storage," Russ said.

"Don't worry, we'll just bring a few clothes and our toothbrushes."

Then Mom and Peaches started talking details.

"We'll fix up the den and you two can stay there," Mom rattled off. "You and Russ can take the train to work — "

"Correction," Peaches cut in. "Russ will take the train to work while I sit around the house and get fat."

"You quit your job?" I gasped. Peaches worked for an advertising firm and was always coming up with wacky ideas for selling toys and weird household products. When they lived in Stoneybrook before, she would try out her latest jingles on us. Janine and I would sing the songs over and over until our parents begged us to be quiet.

"I've always wanted to be a mom," Peaches explained. "I'm going to stay home and enjoy the whole experience."

I could tell by the proud note in her voice that becoming a mother meant an awful lot to her.

After a few more minutes of discussion with Mom, Russ and Peaches agreed that they'd arrive at our house a week from Saturday.

"Only ten more days," I cried as I hung up the extension. "I can't wait."

We tried to return to our dinner but we were

too excited. Mom filled Dad in on the details while Janine and I gushed over what it would be like to have a baby in the house.

"She won't have the baby while she's here," Mom pointed out.

"I know that," I giggled. "But it will be under construction. We'll have so much fun. We can look at those name-the-baby books and baby catalogues, and listen for the heartbeat."

"There's a wonderful video called *The Miracle of Life*," Janine said excitedly. "We can watch that and follow the baby's progress as it develops."

It was just like Janine to view Peaches' visit as some kind of science project. But I didn't mind. For once, science might be really truly interesting.

"Before you both get too carried away," Mom said, pointing at our plates, "let me remind you that your dinners are sitting there growing extremely cold."

I looked down at my mashed meatloaf-peas-and-potatoes. The last thing I wanted to do was eat it. Besides, I was dying to spread the great news. "Look, Mom," I said, picking up my plate, "I'm not really hungry. Is it all right if I put this in the fridge? I can reheat it later."

Dad leaned forward and whispered across the table to Mom. "I think what Claudia is trying to tell us is that she has some important phone calls to make."

I grinned at Dad. "You read my mind."

He waved his napkin at me. "Go ahead. Just don't spend the entire evening on the phone. I'm sure you've got plenty of homework to do."

"I promise I'll be brief."

I think I flew up the stairs. I had a ton of calls to make and not much time. Naturally, the first person I dialed was Stacey.

"Peaches and Russ are moving to Stoneybrook," I shouted the second she picked up. "They're going to be staying with us for a whole month."

"Oh, Claud, that's wonderful!" Stacey gushed. "Is there anything I can do to help?"

"I'm not sure. Peaches will be around a lot. She's quit her job, so she can concentrate on being a mom."

"Maybe she needs some help gathering baby supplies."

"Stacey, you're a genius! I'll call Peaches back and find out what she needs. Maybe I can even make something for her."

I hung up and dialed my aunt. "Peaches, what do you need for the baby?"

"The works," Peaches replied. "A crib, changing table, rocker, night-light, diapers, clothes, towels, washcloths — "

"How about a blanket?" I asked.

"Blankets, a stroller, a playpen," Peaches continued without skipping a beat. "In a word — everything."

I called Mary Anne next. First I broke the big news about my aunt and uncle's move back to Stoneybrook. Then I asked for her help.

"I want to make something for their baby," I explained.

"Gee, Claud, you're much more creative than I am," Mary Anne said. "I'm sure they'd love a painting for the baby's room, or one of those funny mobiles that you make."

"I want this to be something the baby can use," I explained. "I want to knit a blanket."

"I didn't know you knew how to knit," Mary Anne said.

"I don't. I want you to teach me, just like Mimi taught you."

Mimi was special to everyone, but she and Mary Anne had been extra close. This may sound kind of sappy but I thought since Mimi had taught Mary Anne to knit and since Mimi was Peaches' mother, it would be fitting that Mary Anne teach me. The circle would be complete.

"Gee, Claud . . ." Mary Anne hesitated. "A blanket is an awfully big project to start with.

Why don't you do something smaller, like booties?"

"No, I've made up my mind. I really want to knit a blanket."

"Well, okay. How about if we meet for our first lesson next Monday? That way I can have time to find some patterns, and buy whatever we'll need."

After I hung up I dialed the rest of the BSC. Here's what each of them had to say about how we could help Russ and Peaches after they moved to Stoneybrook.

Kristy, the athlete and organizer, declared, "We can all help Peaches stay fit and healthy during her pregnancy. Maybe we should set up a schedule, and each of us can go for walks with her around Stoneybrook."

Mal, our writer, decided she'd create a mother's journal for Peaches. "So she can write down all of the thoughts she's having, and share them with her baby when she's older."

Jessi, the ballerina, wanted to rush right over with some classical music tapes. "Babies can hear in the womb, you know," she said. "Peaches can rest the headphones on her stomach and her baby will develop a taste for wonderful music, and be born with a sense of rhythm and a desire to dance."

"If you speak French to the baby from the

very start," Shannon explained after offering to bring over old beginning French textbooks and tapes, "your new cousin will be bilingual without any effort."

Logan's response was the sweetest. "Your aunt sure is lucky because, if I know you and the rest of the BSC, she won't have to lift a finger. All she'll have to do is sit on her nest and wait for that little egg to hatch."

I even called Dawn in California. "Oh, I just hate you," she cried. "You're going to have so much fun without me."

"Hurry and come back," I urged. "We all miss you."

"I miss you guys, too. The We Love Kids Club is fun, but it's not the BSC."

After I hung up, I thought, *Dawn's right. The Baby-sitters Club is special.* Not only was everyone nearly as thrilled about Russ and Peaches' return to Stoneybrook as I was, they'd even thought of useful ways to help out with the baby. This was going to be an exciting year.

CHAPTER 4

Thursday

I think the frase stuck like glue was invented to describ Nataly Springer. I'm not kiding. For three sollid hours she never left my side. After awile I sugested she call a freind but she told me she didnt have any.

"**H**ow about Karen Brewer?" I asked. "Didn't you stay with her when your parents went away?"

Natalie tugged at her sock, which was drooping around her ankle. "That was when Grandpa died. Karen's nice to me, but her real friends are Hannie and Nancy. They're the Three Muthketeers."

Natalie spoke so softly that at first I hadn't noticed she had a lisp. But when she said, "Muthketeers," I knew for certain.

"Well, there must be someone from your class at school we could call to come play with you."

Natalie shrugged. "Nobody I can think of."

This was a little odd. I thought back to when I was in second grade. I had spent most of my time with Kristy or Mary Anne. And if they were busy, I had known a lot of other kids I could call. Natalie sounded like she didn't have one single friend.

"Is there anyone that you'd like to be your friend?"

Natalie looked up at me with crooked glasses and a big smile. "You. I'd like it if you were my friend."

"Well, of course, I'll be your friend," I said, feeling flattered. And just to show Natalie I meant it, I gave her a big hug. "See? Now we're pals."

"Can we pretend that we're the Two Musketeers?" she asked.

"Of course," I said, saluting her with a pretend sword. "One for all. And all for one."

"Oh, boy." Natalie hopped up and down and both socks drooped back around her ankles. "Wait till Karen Brewer hears that I have a friend who's in eighth grade. She'll be so jealous!"

It didn't really sink in until later, after we'd left Elm Street and circled the neighborhood together, how much my being her friend meant to Natalie. Every time we passed any other kid, Natalie'd slip her hand into mine and say, really loudly, "Claudia, I'm so glad you're my friend."

When we got to Carle Playground she announced, "Now we should play Lovely Ladies."

Lovely Ladies, I remembered, was one of Karen Brewer's favorite games, but I wasn't sure I could recall the rules. "All right, Natalie, how do we play?"

Natalie looked confused for a second. Hmm. Maybe she had never even played it herself, but had only watched Karen and her friends playing it. I decided to forge ahead.

Clasping my hands delicately in front of me, I pretended to be a very fancy lady. "My, my, Natalie," I said in a high-pitched voice, "isn't it an exquisite day?"

Natalie imitated my movements and, in her own piping voice, lisped, "Yes, it's just beautiful. A perfect day to walk my five poodles."

"Oh? Now you have five?" I raised one eyebrow. "And what, may I ask, is the new one's name?"

"Pierre," she answered. "Naturally."

"That's right. You name all of your poodles Pierre. I should have remembered."

Natalie dabbed at her eyes with the corner of her T-shirt and pretended to cry. "Pierre was my first husband. I'll never forget him."

Several kids had gathered on the playground to stare at us.

"What are they? Nuts?" one little kid asked his older brother.

I turned around and said, "We're not nuts, we're Lovely Ladies."

The older boy nodded down at his brother. "That proves it. They're nuts."

"Come along, Natalie," I declared. "I can see we're not wanted here." Taking hands, we stood up and walked away from those boys and out of the park with all the dignity we could muster. But the second we were around the corner, we burst out laughing. Natalie was laughing so hard she made a little snort every time she caught her breath.

"Did you see the (snort) look on that kid's face?" she gasped. "He really thought we were (snort) nuts (snort, snort)!"

"I can just hear them telling their parents that two Lovely Ladies have escaped from the looney bin," I said, giggling. "Then their parents will think *they're* crazy."

Natalie couldn't even reply. She just laughed. "Snort! Snort! Snort!"

When we got back to Natalie's, I made us a sandwich of peanut butter, bananas, and mayonnaise. It looks kind of gross but really tastes great. Natalie thought so, too.

"This is my most favorite sandwich I've ever eaten," Natalie said as she munched away. "You sure are a good cook, Claudia."

"Call me Claud," I told her. "A lot of my friends call me that."

Natalie gave me an ear-to-ear grin that was pretty disgusting, considering the peanut butter and bananas stuck to her teeth. "All right, Claud. And you can call me Nat."

I smiled back (keeping my lips together). "It's a deal."

When I got home that afternoon, the Kishi household was in complete turmoil. Dad and Mom had moved some of the furniture out of the den and into the living room to make room for a bed for Peaches and Russ. One of the small dressers from our upstairs closet was sitting at the foot of the stairs, along with a bedside lamp from the garage. We spent the evening rearranging the house, and I didn't have time to think about Natalie. In fact, I forgot all about her until Friday afternoon, when I came home from school. The phone rang the instant I walked through the front door.

"Hi, Claud. How was school?"

She didn't say who she was but I recognized the lisp.

"Hi, Nat," I said. "School was pretty good." I wasn't going to go into details with a second-grader, but actually, my classes had been hard. It was my fault because I wasn't really concentrating. I'd spent the day making a mental list of the items we still needed for Russ and Peaches' room. "How was your school day?"

"The same," Natalie said in her soft little voice.

"Did you meet any new kids today?" I asked, remembering our conversation about friends.

"No, but I did tell Karen Brewer that you were my friend and that we are the Two Musketeers now."

"What did she think?"

"She didn't believe me. She said you were

Stacey's best friend. Who is Stacey?"

"Stacey McGill *is* my best friend. We're in the Baby-sitters Club together. But you know, a person can have a lot of friends."

"Well, I just wanted to call to make sure you were still my friend."

"Don't worry, Natalie," I said. "I'm still your friend."

I thought it was sweet that Natalie had called and that our friendship meant so much to her. I even mentioned it that afternoon at the BSC meeting.

"She's not exactly Miss Popularity," I explained to those in the club who hadn't met her. "I mean, she looks a little unkempt. Her socks droop around her ankles, her glasses are always a bit crooked on her nose, and her hair is kind of a mess. But she's very sweet."

"I remember Karen was worried about her, because Natalie didn't seem to have any friends," Kristy said.

"That's right. She really doesn't," I replied. "I promised to be her friend and that totally made her day."

"Poor Natalie," Mary Anne said with a little sniff. (Remember, I told you she cries at TV commercials.) "I wish there was something we could do to help her."

The phone rang before anybody could come up with a solution to Natalie's problem. And then it rang again. And again. In twenty minutes, eight parents called, and by the end of the meeting we had all booked jobs.

The next day was Saturday — exactly one week before Peaches and Russ would arrive. One week doesn't seem like very long. But when you are counting the hours and minutes, it is. I figured it would make the time go faster if I kept really busy.

I found Mom's work list on the kitchen table. Here's what it said:

Things to do before Peaches and Russ arrive

1. *Rake leaves.*
2. *Air out curtains.*
3. *Shake out rug.*
4. *Fix lampshade.*
5. *Put better support under mattress.*
6. *Clean entire house, top to bottom !!!!*

I decided I could probably help with the first three items, and most definitely with the last one. It was a beautiful fall morning, so I grabbed a rake from the garage and headed for the front yard. Mom was already outside, beating the rug (so much for item three).

I had just raked the leaves into three large piles when I heard the sound of a bicycle bell.

Brring! Brring!

"Hi, Claud. What are you doing?"

I looked up to see Natalie Springer, wearing a jean jumper, turtleneck top . . . and saggy socks. She was grinning at me from the sidewalk.

"Hi, Nat. We're doing major housecleaning today, inside and — " I held up my rake. "Out."

"Can I help?" Natalie asked, setting her bike down on its side by one of the leaf piles. "I like to clean."

I had to think about it for a second. On one hand, I didn't know what Natalie was really capable of doing. On the other, it would be nice to have some company while I scrubbed the bathroom and kitchen floors.

"Sure, if it's okay with your mom," I said, putting my rake in the garage. "Come on, let's go call her."

Of course, Mrs. Springer was delighted that I was spending time with Natalie. "Keep her for as long as you like," she said. "Natalie is so happy that you're her friend."

Actually, Natalie was more than just good company. She helped squeeze out the sponge mop and refill the bucket of water when I was cleaning the floors. And she did a pretty decent job of dusting the living room. I only had to do a few touch-ups.

Three hours later, we'd eaten lunch and it was time for Natalie to go home. She hugged me and said, "Gee, Claud, that was really fun. Can we do it again soon?"

It's hard for me to think of cleaning as fun, but if Natalie found it that entertaining, I wasn't about to change her mind. So I put on a perky smile and said, "I hope so!"

Unfortunately, Natalie took that to mean that we would be cleaning often. In fact, she called every day for the next week to check on it. "How's your house now?" she would ask. "Has it gotten dirty yet?"

I thought it was cute.

CHAPTER 5

"They're here!" I shouted on Saturday morning. "Peaches and Russ are here!"

I watched their green Volvo station wagon creep up the street. I think Russ was driving slowly because it was packed to the brim. Bedspreads, suitcases, and boxes filled the rear of the car and several more boxes were tied onto the roof.

Honk! Honk!

Russ hit the horn as they pulled into our driveway. Peaches was out of the car before he'd even turned off the engine. She waved her arms and called, "Don't panic! We're only staying a month. Pillows take up a lot of space, and those boxes are filled with my office supplies."

I giggled and gave Peaches a gentle hug. I was afraid to squeeze her too hard because of the baby but Peaches didn't seem to be concerned. She swooped me into a tight hug.

Then Russ wrapped his arms around the two of us. (Russ and Peaches never miss a chance to hug people. That's one of the best things about them.)

"Hey, Claud," Russ said. "Would you mind helping me unload?"

I shrugged. "That's why I'm here. Hand me a couple of boxes."

Peaches started to reach for a suitcase in the backseat but Russ leaped in front of her, barring the car door. "No way, little mother. You can carry your purse or the pillows, and maybe a small blanket, but that's it. Doctor's orders."

Peaches rolled her eyes at me. "The doctor happened to mention to Russ that I should be careful to not lift anything heavy, like a piano or a bus. Now Russ won't leave me alone. This morning he snatched a gallon of milk out of my hands and said, 'That's it. From here on out, we're buying half pints.' "

I thought it was awfully sweet that Russ was so concerned. But I could see how it might bug Peaches, who is very independent and likes to do everything herself.

It took a little while to get all of the boxes and suitcases out of the car. I helped Peaches hang up their clothes in the downstairs closet while Dad and Russ moved the office supplies into the garage.

"You two are so great," Peaches cooed

when she saw the fresh flowers Janine and I had picked that morning and set in a vase beside their bed. "I'm going to love staying here. It'll be like one big slumber party."

"Lunchtime," Mom called from the kitchen. She sounded calm, but I knew that two hours earlier she had been in a complete tizzy over what to serve for the meal. "We need to eat foods high in iron and protein for the baby and for Peaches," she'd declared, frantically thumbing through her recipe file.

Three cookbooks and one mad dash to the grocery store later, she was serving up a very healthy (and, okay, I'll admit it, delicious) lunch of spinach salad, fresh tomato soup, and melon slices.

"That was simply scrumptious," Peaches said as she dabbed her lips with a napkin. "You shouldn't have gone to so much trouble. I would have just sent out for a pizza."

Mom thanked her, adding, "I want to make sure you have the best diet for a mother-to-be."

"And speaking of mothers and babies, and all of those wonderful subjects," Peaches said, looking around the table with a grin. "Who would like to go shopping with me? I'm in the mood to buy baby furniture."

My hand shot up into the air. "Take me. Oh, *please* take me!"

Peaches pulled a shopping list out of her pocket and held it up for us to see. "Russ and I pored over issue after issue of *Consumer Reports* to find the most recommended baby items and, after many late nights, we finally came up with the definitive shopping list. We've even talked to a few stores, who said they'd hold our purchases until we can move into our house."

"Did you call Baby and Company?" I asked.

Peaches grinned. "They were first on my list."

After helping Mom with the dishes, Peaches and I headed downtown to Baby and Company. It's my favorite baby store, completely devoted to baby clothes and furniture. Karen Brewer once called it a baby museum. And she's right. If it has anything at all to do with babies, they have it.

Peaches and I spent a full two hours in there. By the time we finished, I was exhausted, not from the actual shopping but from going, "Oooh, look! Isn't this darling!" every two seconds. We started *ooh!*-ing and *ah!*-ing before we even made it through the door. The window display was a little bedroom decorated to look like a baby animal jungle, including a huge stuffed giraffe. It was adorable.

"Let's start with the big things," Peaches

said, reading from her list. "Crib, changing table, rocker, baby swing, and infant car seat."

The crib we chose was painted white, with graceful arches at each end and drawers along the bottom, beneath the mattress. Each crib had a girl's name. This one was called a Mary Catherine. (I think it was the most expensive one in the store.) So, naturally, Peaches had to choose the Mary Catherine glider rocker and Mary Catherine changing table to match.

Of course, while we were picking cribs and rockers we had to pick out crib bumpers, sheets, the bed ruffle, and matching rocker cushions. We thumbed through catalog after catalog of designer baby things. Eventually, Peaches picked out a pattern of pastel bears holding hands (or I guess I should say, paws), surrounded by stars, rainbows, and soft pink clouds. The bears were pink and blue and lime green and peach, and wore jackets and hats. There was even a little bear mobile to match the sheets and comforter.

I couldn't get over how much a person has to think about to get ready for a new baby. A mattress protector, a changing table pad, a dresser that a child couldn't tip over, and a diaper pail that the child couldn't open by herself. Luckily Baby and Company had complete "childproofing" kits that included electrical outlet guards, cupboard and toilet seat locks, and doorknob covers. Just looking at all you needed to make a house safe for a baby made me feel a little nervous.

When we had the bedroom fitted out, we moved on to other large equipment. The car seat and swing were easy. Peaches just referred to her *Consumer Reports* list. We did have to choose between "Rock-a-bye Baby" and "Frére Jacques" for the tune the baby swing would play.

"It's a matter of choosing one you won't mind listening to a few thousand times," the saleslady said, with a twinkle in her eye.

"The bear mobile already plays 'Rock-a-bye Baby,' " I pointed out to Peaches. "And I bet people will give you plenty of wind-up toys and music boxes that play that song, too."

Peaches patted me on the shoulder. "You sold me. We'll take 'Frére Jacques.' "

Then we moved on to my favorite section — the baby clothes. (Major *ooh! ah!* time.)

"We don't know yet whether it's going to be a girl or a boy," Peaches said. "But I've always hated that old 'Girls have to wear pink, and boys have to wear blue' routine. Why don't we each pick out a couple of outfits we like in the newborn to six month size, and take it from there?"

"Everything is so tiny. It's just too cute for

words," I said as I held up sleeper after sleeper.

"Look at these socks!" Peaches held up a pink ruffled sock that could have fit on her thumb. "It's hard to believe a baby's foot could be so small."

Just talking about how little and precious a baby is brought tears to our eyes. I would have felt silly crying in any other store, but I could tell by the saleslady's reaction that she was used to it. Even *her* eyes looked a little misty.

Peaches had the saleslady ring everything up (the sales ticket was two feet long!) and made arrangements for the furniture, the car seat, and the other big items to be delivered later, to the new house. But we both agreed that we wanted to take the baby clothes with us so that we could *ooh!* and *ahh!* with Russ, Mom, Dad, and Janine back at home.

While Peaches was signing the credit card form at the cash register, I looked at baby blankets. Several of the ones on display had been knit by hand. They were just beautiful. I made a mental note of one in particular, a pale lavender throw laced with delicate little designs at the top and bottom. I knew I wanted Mary Anne to help me knit a blanket like that one.

We hauled the packages out to the car and

tossed them in the back. As Peaches settled in behind the wheel she turned to me and said, "That was a blast. What should we do now?"

"Do?" Frankly, I was kind of tired from our shopping spree and I had figured Peaches would be completely worn out. I remember Mrs. Newton was always taking naps when she was pregnant.

"I'm too excited to just go home," Peaches said as she started the engine. "What do you say we go to the movies?"

"I'd love to," I said, "but . . ."

"But what?" Peaches demanded.

"I have homework."

"Homework on a Saturday?" Peaches waved one hand at me. "You've got to be kidding. That's what Sundays are for."

I knew that if I waited until Sunday to do my homework, I might not finish it. Then Monday would roll around and I'd be in a panic. Besides, I had a baby-sitting job on Sunday.

"I'm supposed to sit for the Barretts tomorrow," I explained.

"So take your homework with you." Peaches suggested. "Or get up early tomorrow morning and I'll help you. And what I don't know, Russ can fill in. *Or* — do it tonight."

Peaches was very convincing. I have to admit, I love spur of the moment decisions and after all, it *was* Saturday. Most kids in America go out and have fun on Saturdays.

"Okay." I grinned. "You sold me. Let's go to the movies."

We hurriedly bought a newspaper to see what movies were playing. Peaches is so crazy. She suggested we just close our eyes, point to a movie ad, then go see whatever movie the ad was for. Want to hear something amazing? Peaches picked *Bringing Up Baby*, an old movie playing at this tiny little theatre that shows only old movies and foreign films. We both decided it was a major good luck sign.

The movie was really funny. You see, it stars Katharine Hepburn and Cary Grant. Katharine Hepburn is this rich girl who falls in love with Cary Grant, who plays a crazy dinosaur scientist (Peaches said they're called paleontologists). Here's the really silly part: Baby isn't a baby at all. Baby is the name of her pet leopard. We had a terrific time gorging ourselves on popcorn from an old-fashioned popcorn machine they had in the lobby, plus two boxes of Junior Mints (my choice), and an ice cream bar (Peaches's choice). It was a great afternoon!

When we finally pulled into my driveway, we found Natalie Springer sitting on the front stoop. She had her chin in her hands and was looking really dejected.

"Hi, Natalie! What are you doing here?" I called from behind my load of packages.

"I've been waiting for you to come home and play with me," she replied.

"Play with you?" I opened the front door for Peaches, who carried her packages inside to her room. Then I set my own bags by the front closet and returned to Natalie. "How long have you been sitting there?"

Natalie, whose glasses were more crooked than usual, shrugged. "A few minutes, but it feels like hours."

"Look, Natalie," I said, trying to be gentle, "I'd like to play with you but I can't right now. I have to do my homework."

"Homework?" She scrunched up her nose. "On Saturday?"

Now Natalie was sounding like Peaches! "I really have a lot of homework to do," I said, more firmly this time. "And if I played with you, it might not get done. I'll walk you home, and maybe we can set up a date to play another time."

"You don't have to walk me home," Natalie said with a loud sniff. "I can go by myself."

"Well, okay," I said. "But if you don't mind, I'll walk you to the corner."

Natalie really looked miserable as she headed down Elm Street. Her shoulders were hunched over and she stared at the sidewalk the entire way. I felt sorry for her, but I knew I had to hit the books. I was not about to get into trouble over my schoolwork.

Sunday

Sunday was my turn to be Natalie's friend. Sorry, Claud, but it seems that Natalie attaches herself to whoever is there. I mean, this girl has a serious gap in the friendship department. I think we should discuss this at the next meeting. Okay, Kristy? Maybe you'll have one of your great ideas and help us solve Natalie's problem.

Stacey had never met Natalie before, but you wouldn't have known it from the way Natalie greeted her at the door.

"Stacey! I'm *so* glad you're here. Come on in. Want a peanut butter, mayonnaise, and banana sandwich?"

Stacey happens to hate that combination but she didn't tell Natalie that. Instead she said, "I see Claud's been cooking for you. That's her favorite sandwich. But it's not really mine."

"What's your favorite?" Natalie asked.

"I like lettuce, tomato, and cheese sandwiches on whole wheat bread," Stacey said. "Sometimes I just eat lettuce and tomato without the cheese. It tastes great, and it's really healthy, too."

"That's my favorite kind of sandwich, too," Natalie said, opening the refrigerator door. "You want to make one?"

It was about two o'clock, and Stacey had already eaten lunch. "I'm not really hungry right now," she said, "but if you want to eat something, I'll fix you one."

Natalie shut the refrigerator door. "I guess I'm not hungry either."

"Then why don't we do something together?" Stacey suggested. "We could make a fort, or play dolls — whatever you like."

"You'll really play with me?" Natalie asked, shoving her glasses up on her nose.

"Of course." Stacey smiled. "That's what I'm here for. To make sure you're safe and looked after, but also to play with you and have fun."

"Does that mean you'll be my friend?" Natalie asked.

Stacey knew that Natalie had asked to be my best friend, and a tiny warning bell went off in her head. Instead of immediately answering yes, the way I had done, she said, "It's nice to have friends, isn't it, Natalie?"

Natalie nodded vigorously.

"Why don't you invite some of your friends over and we can all play together?"

Natalie pulled on the knee sock drooping around her ankle. "I don't have any friends."

Stacey knew that Natalie had said the same thing to me, but she still had a hard time believing it.

"Surely you must have friends at school."

"Not really."

"How about in the neighborhood?"

"Nope."

"Nobody at all?" Stacey asked.

Natalie squinched one eye shut. "Claudia is my friend. But that's it."

Stacey cocked her head. "I bet you have

more friends than you think. Why don't we go outside and see."

Natalie looked up at her curiously. "What will we do outside?"

"We'll play on your porch and see if any potential friends come along."

Natalie shrugged her shoulders. "Okay."

Stacey grabbed her Kid-Kit and led Natalie out on' the front porch. They sat down cross-legged, [and opened] her decorated box.

"W[ant to play] jacks?" she asked, taking [out the jacks and] spilling the ball and ja[cks on the flo]or. "That's always fun."

"I [sure do," Natalie] replied. "It's my favorit[e game!]

Sta[cey began to] notice a pattern. Wha[tever she did, Nat]alie liked. In fact, it insta[ntly became her favo]rite thing. *I guess it coul[d be worse,* Stacey th]ought. "She could hate everything I like."

Stacey tossed the ball in the air and started to scoop up her jacks when someone shouted from the street.

"Hi, Stacey!"

It was Corrie Addison. She was riding bikes with Haley Braddock.

"Hi, you guys," Stacey called. "What are you up to?"

"We're seeing how far we can coast without pedaling," Corrie replied.

"We've already gone two whole blocks," Haley added.

Stacey turned to Natalie. "Would you like to play with Haley and Corrie?"

"They're in the fourth grade," Natalie said simply. "And besides, Haley's best friends with Vanessa Pike. And Corrie is usually with her brother."

None of those seemed like a very good reason not to play with them, but Stacey kept her mouth shut. A few minutes later, a brown-haired girl came by on skates. She stuck out her tongue at Natalie as she went past the house.

"Who was that?" Stacey asked. "Not that she looks very friendly."

"She's in my class at school." Natalie crinkled her nose. "Her name's Leslie Morris and I don't like her at all. Besides she's already friends with Pamela Harding and Jannie Gilbert."

"What about those kids?" Stacey pointed across the street to a boy and girl pulling a red wagon filled with dirt.

"That's Leif and Lindsey," Natalie replied. "They live on Rockville Court. But they're best friends."

The way Natalie talked, it sounded like all of the friends in the world were spoken for. She didn't seem to understand that you could be friends with more than one person. Stacey decided she'd talk to me about this friendship problem later. In the meantime, Natalie looked like she could use some cheering up. Stacey scooped up the remaining jacks and dropped them in her Kid-Kit. Then she stood up.

"Come on, Natalie." Stacey held out her hand. "There's someone I'd like you to meet."

Natalie slipped her hand into Stacey's and smiled. "Who is it?"

"I'm not telling," Stacey said mysteriously. "But I'll give you a hint. He has a pink nose and big ears, and he can jump pretty high."

"Gee." Natalie tugged at her sock again. "I don't know anybody who looks like that. He sounds weird."

Stacey smiled. "He's not weird and he's really not a kid."

After scribbling a note to Mrs. Springer, Stacey grabbed a few items from the refrigerator and then they headed for Brenner field. Stacey kept Natalie guessing the entire way.

"Is it your dad?" Natalie asked. "Does he have funny ears and a pink nose?"

Stacey laughed. "His ears could be called funny, but his nose is definitely not pink."

"If it's not a kid and not a grown-up," Natalie said, pushing up her glasses, "then it can't be a person."

"Right!"

By now they'd arrived. Stacey led the way over to a large rock standing at one end of the field. Then she put her finger to her lips and whispered, "Now we have to keep really quiet or we'll scare Peter away."

"Peter? His name is Peter?" Natalie whispered excitedly. "Where is he?"

Stacey pointed to a low hedge a few feet from the big rock. "He's usually hiding in there."

"Under that bush? What could hide there?"

Stacey didn't have to answer, because at that moment a fluffy brown-and-white rabbit stuck his head out of the bushes. He raised his head, wiggled his nose several times, then hopped cautiously into the open.

"It's a bunny!" Natalie cried with glee. "Oh, Stacey, he's so cute. Can we pet him?"

"Wait a minute." Stacey dug in the pocket of her jacket and produced the two carrots she'd taken from the Springers' refrigerator. "Here. Now you can feed him. But don't move too fast. We don't want to scare Peter away."

Natalie held her carrot out in front of her and slowly walked toward the small rabbit.

"Is he someone's pet?" she whispered back over her shoulder.

"I don't think so," Stacey said. "I think he's a wild bunny that's used to having a lot of kids around. Peter's kind of the neighborhood's pet. But he also makes a very nice friend."

Natalie knelt down in front of the rabbit, who watched her carefully. Slowly she placed the carrot on the grass in front of the bunny. Peter took two hops forward and nibbled on the tip of the carrot with his big front teeth.

"Look!" Natalie whispered, as Peter took another crunchy bite. "He's not afraid of me. He's my friend."

Stacey leaned her back against the big rock while she watched Natalie. Natalie seemed like a sweet little kid. It just didn't make sense for her not to have any friends. Time to find out more about Natalie, Stacey decided. That night after dinner, before she started her homework, Stacey called me to talk about Natalie's problem.

"Do you think she really doesn't have any friends, or is she just saying that to get our sympathy?" Stacey asked.

"I think she really doesn't have anyone," I replied. "She's been over here a lot during the past week."

"She comes over to your house?"

"Yeah, and not only that, she calls me after she gets home. Last night she called just to say goodnight, sleep tight."

"Oh, that's sweet," Stacey said.

I agreed. "But I don't like having to tell her to go home all the time. And now that Peaches is here, I have even less time to spend with Natalie than before."

"Besides, Natalie needs her own friends," Stacey added. "We're baby-sitters, and we need to make that clear. I mean, imagine what it'd be like if all of our charges dropped by our homes or called us all the time."

"Yikes! We'd never have any time to ourselves. We'd have to hide out — "

"Maybe even wear disguises." Stacey chuckled.

"We'd have to have unlisted phone numbers and secret code names," I added. "It would be totally ridiculous."

We laughed, but then Stacey said in as serious a voice as was possible, "It's time we talked to the BSC about this."

I agreed. "I'll bring it up first thing on Monday."

CHAPTER 7

"Anybody home?" I called as I came through the front door Monday afternoon. I'd raced home from school and I was out of breath. "Peaches?" I called cautiously into the den. "Are you in there?"

No answer. Phew. Today was my first knitting lesson, and I didn't want Peaches to know anything about it. Moments later, the doorbell rang.

"Come on in, Mary Anne," I said, throwing open the front door. "The coast is clear."

Mary Anne and I hurried up the stairs. We had a lot to do before the BSC meeting at five-thirty. Mary Anne was carrying a large over-stuffed tapestry bag in one hand and a couple of pattern books in the other. She dumped everything on my bed.

"I think I've brought everything we need for your first lesson," she said.

I lifted up my mattress and pulled out a

sketch I had done of the blanket I'd seen at Baby and Company. "This is the blanket I want to knit," I explained.

Mary Anne looked at the sketch and gasped. "Oh, Claudia, it's very pretty, but . . ."

"But what?" I sat on the bed next to Mary Anne and peered over her shoulder at my drawing.

"It's a really complicated pattern. I don't even think *I* could knit it, let alone teach you how to do it."

"I really had my heart set on that one." I sighed.

"Why don't we look at my patterns?" Mary Anne reached for the books she'd brought. "Maybe we can find something like it."

We flipped through several books and finally settled on one of the simpler patterns.

"This is a good one," Mary Anne said firmly, tapping her finger on the picture in the magazine. "It has a block pattern, but you only need to knit and purl."

I threw my hands in the air. "Well, you've already lost me."

Mary Anne laughed. "I know it sounds like a foreign language right now, but pretty soon you'll be saying 'knit one, purl two' in your sleep."

Then she opened the tapestry bag and pulled out several skeins of pale lavender yarn. "Is this the color you wanted?" she asked.

"It's perfect." I held the soft yarn to my face. "Lavender is good when you don't know if it's going to be a boy or a girl. Plus, it matches the crib bumpers beautifully."

Next Mary Anne pulled out two metal needles from her bag and handed them to me. "Careful," she said, in her best baby-sitter's voice. "Points down, Claudia. You could put your eye out."

"I didn't realize knitting was such a dangerous hobby." I giggled.

She gestured to the yarn and the needles. "That's all you need. Now if you can knit and purl, and follow the directions, you'll have a beautiful blanket."

"Great!" I picked up the loose end of the yarn and held it up to the needles. "What do I do first? Make some kind of square knot on one of the needles?"

"Not exactly. Here." Mary Anne reached for the needles and yarn. "I'll make it easy for you, and cast on."

"Cast on?" I repeated. "I thought I was knitting, not fishing."

"Watch." Mary Anne held a needle in one hand and looped the yarn around it. Her hands moved so fast that I could barely tell what she was doing. She counted under her breath as she worked to one hundred and twenty-five. Less than two minutes later, she held up the needle with the yarn attached to it. "There. Now you're ready to begin."

"You better back up a minute," I said, suddenly having second thoughts about this whole knitting business. "I have no idea what you just did."

"Okay. How about if I do the first row," Mary Anne suggested. "I'll go very slowly, so you can follow what I'm doing. Then you can do the second row."

I watched her like a hawk. First she stuck the point of the needle under one of the loops. Then she wrapped the yarn around the end of the needle, did a little over-and-under movement and suddenly the yarn was on the other needle. She worked her way across the yarn she'd already attached to the needles, and then handed the knitting to me. "Now you try."

"Oh, boy." I was so nervous I could barely hold the needles. "It's like trying to use those big kindergarten pencils," I muttered as I stuck one needle into the loop.

"Careful!" Mary Anne warned. "Or the yarn will slip off your other — "

She didn't finish because the yarn not only slipped off that needle but, when I dove to pick it up, it slid off the other, too.

"Oh, no," I cried. "My loops are gone."

Mary Anne laughed gently. "I'll put your 'loops' back on for you, but this time watch carefully. I have a feeling you're going to be doing this a lot."

"Maybe those needles are too slippery," I said as Mary Anne started the poke-and-loop routine again. "Maybe I could find some made out of wood."

"Or sandpaper?" Mary Anne giggled. "That would keep the yarn from slipping."

I tried to knit again and again. Each time I'd lose the loop, or "drop the stitch" (as Mary Anne said), or just create a great big knot. "Ooooh!" I blew a strand of hair off my forehead. "This is really frustrating."

Mary Anne sat back with her arms folded across her chest, smiling smugly. "Actually, it's kind of fun to see you looking a little uncoordinated."

"Fun?" I felt like throwing the ball of yarn at her. Instead I pointed the needles at her and demanded, "What so fun about it?"

Mary Anne covered her mouth, trying to stop laughing. "I'm sorry, Claud, but you are usually Miss Total Artist — always making perfect jewelry and perfect sculptures. It's just nice to know that even you have difficulty with some creative things."

"Hmmph. I bet I wouldn't have any difficulty tossing this yarn and those books right out the window," I threatened, reaching for Mary Anne's tapestry bag.

"Stop!" Mary Anne held up both hands. "I promise not to laugh anymore. On one condition."

"What's that?"

"That you try to knit one whole row before the meeting begins."

The meeting? I'd forgotten all about it. I checked my clock and then looked at the bed in dismay. The meeting was due to start in just ten minutes, and yarn and pattern books were strewn everywhere.

"Okay," I said. "I'll knit. If you'll pick up."

"It's a deal."

Quickly Mary Anne stacked all the pattern books in a neat pile on my desk. Then she carefully tucked the blanket drawing back under the mattress. After that she dropped the extra balls of yarn into her tapestry bag.

"How are you doing?" she asked when she'd finished.

"Well, I've done half a row," I said, still concentrating on my work. "At this rate, Peaches' baby should get this blanket in time for her high school graduation."

"Knock! Knock!" Stacey stuck her head in my room. "Is this a private party, or can anybody join?"

"Come on in!" Boy, was I relieved to see Stacey. I really did want to learn to knit, but I was fast reaching burnout on my first lesson.

"What's going on?" Stacey asked as she took her usual position on my bed.

I tucked my first efforts into the tapestry bag and then turned to grin at Stacey. "Mary Anne's been needling me for the last half hour."

Mary Anne giggled at my joke and added, "Yeah, and Claud's been keeping me in stitches."

Stacey raised one eyebrow at me. "Those are supposed to be knitting jokes, right? You can't pull the wool over my eyes."

Luckily for all of us, Kristy arrived before anyone could make another crack about being knit-picky or spinning yarns. Shannon, Mal, and Jessi were right behind her.

Kristy called our meeting to order at exactly five-thirty (of course), and then went right to the point. "I know some of you want to talk about our new charge, Natalie Springer, so, Claudia, why don't you start?"

I took a deep breath. "You guys probably remember that when I sat for Natalie last week, she asked me to be her friend. I said, of course I'd be her friend. I mean, that's not such an unusual thing for a little kid to say. But ever since, she hasn't stopped calling me.

71

Now she drops by the house all the time and stays for hours. I'm not sure what to do about it. It's not that I mind her company; I just think she should be playing with kids her own age."

"Doesn't she know any neighbor kids she could play with?" Mallory asked.

Stacey answered that question. "She knows who the neighbor kids are, but she has a thousand excuses for why she can't play with them. She asked me to be her friend, too. But after hearing about Claud's experience, I was a little more cautious in responding to her."

Kristy pushed up her visor. "I called Karen last night and asked her about Natalie. Karen says that Natalie is kind of the outcast in her class. It's not that the kids are mean to her. It's just that they don't notice her."

"That's even worse," I said, wincing.

"What can we do about it?" Jessi asked.

Kristy shrugged. "We'll just have to find Natalie some friends her own age."

"But how?" Mal asked.

"What if we had a party?" Mary Anne suggested. "And each one of us invited a friend for her?"

"Good idea," Kristy said, nodding. "But we need more than that. A bigger, overall plan. Kind of a campaign."

"A friendship campaign?" Shannon repeated. "That sounds good. Let's come up with a list of ideas to make it work."

Mary Anne held up her pen. "Fire away."

Mal raised her hand. (She and Jessi still do that. I think it's a habit from school.) "What if every time we sit for Natalie, we make arrangements to invite someone over for her to play with?"

"We could suggest that she join some activities that other charges are involved in," I said. "Like art classes — "

"Or dance classes," Jessi added.

Mal raised her hand again. "I could ask the triplets to invite her to join their kickball team."

"Maybe Natalie could work on a junior fundraising drive for some charity," Stacey suggested. "Or even lead one. The Diabetes Association is about to launch their fall campaign. If Natalie helped out, she'd be sure to meet people."

Mary Anne neatly printed everyone's suggestions in the notebook. Then the phone started ringing. After we'd assigned our sitting jobs, Kristy took another look at the list. "This is a great start, you guys. If we really do all of these things, Natalie should be the most popular girl in Stoneybrook."

The phone rang one last time before the meeting ended, and Jessi answered.

"Hello, Mrs. Springer," she said in an overly

loud voice. That quieted everyone. "We were just talking about Natalie, and how much we like her."

Jessi listened and nodded several times.

"You need a sitter for Natalie after school on Wednesday?"

There was a hasty discussion among the rest of us.

"Let me take this job," Shannon whispered. "I'd like to try my hand at the Friendship Campaign."

Usually we take the information about a job, and then call the client back to tell them who'll be sitting, but we were all eager to start helping Natalie, so Mary Anne checked the book and nodded her approval. Kristy gestured to Jessi that Shannon would take the job.

"Shannon Kilbourne will be there Wednesday afternoon at four on the dot," Jessi said to Mrs. Springer.

After Jessi had hung up the phone, Kristy folded her arms and grinned at us. "The Friendship Campaign is off and running!"

CHAPTER 8

Homework. Yuck. It was Tuesday afternoon, and I had a huge stack of books on my desk. One from each class. I had to write a book report for English (which meant that I also had to finish reading a book). I was supposed to complete a worksheet for math class, and read two chapters for science. My art project waited, untouched, in the corner. It was almost too much. I put my head on my desk, preparing for the long hours ahead of me.

"Knock, knock." Peaches stuck her head in my room. "Oops, sorry. I didn't realize you were napping."

I raised my head. "No. Come on in. I'm not napping. I'm thinking."

"That makes two of us." Peaches came into the room and perched on the edge of my bed. "And I'm tired of it. I want to do something."

"I know what I have to do," I said with a groan. "Homework."

Peaches wrinkled her nose. "That's no fun. Why don't you do it later and come with me?"

"Where are you going?"

"To the store. I was downstairs looking at cookbooks, trying to plan out a nutritious diet for the baby and me, and suddenly I was famished."

"I can understand that," I said, hungrily eyeing the bag of Mallomars I had stashed between two books on the shelf above my desk.

"Looking at all of those wonderful cookbooks gave me an idea," Peaches continued. "I thought, why not make a gourmet dinner, complete with fancy hors d'oeuvres and a scrumptious, ultra-rich, triple chocolate dessert."

She'd said the magic word — *chocolate*. I spun in my chair. "When were you going to do all of this?"

"Tonight. Now." Peaches leapt to her feet and grabbed one of my hands. "But I can't do it alone and there's no one else here."

"What about Janine?" I asked. "She likes to cook."

Peaches shook her head. "Janine's long gone. She went off with her boyfriend. They said something about hamburgers and the library. Not my idea of an exciting date, but . . ."

I looked back at my stack of books. The last thing on earth I wanted to do was homework, but I needed to do it. I really did.

Peaches tugged on my arm. "Come on, Claud," she pleaded. "It'll be fun."

"But my homework," I protested weakly.

"You can do that later. I'll help you."

I remembered that the last time she'd promised to help, a good movie had come on television that she and Russ wanted to watch. I hadn't had the heart to butt in and ask them to help me. But maybe this time would be different.

"Okay," I said. "Just this once. I really can't make a habit of it. You know what my grades are like."

"Hooray!" Peaches jumped with one fist in the air, like a cheerleader. "Come on. This will be a hoot."

I soon forgot about my homework as we prepared for the feast of the century, as Peaches called it. First she spread out her cookbooks and we made up a hasty shopping list from the recipes she'd chosen. Then we hopped in her car and took off. It was the craziest shopping trip I'd ever been on.

"First stop," Peaches announced as we pulled up in front of a tiny shop with a newly shingled roof. "In Good Taste."

"I've never been here," I said, glancing at

the display of cans of imported olive oil and brightly colored bins of pasta in the window. "What is it — some kind of gourmet shop?"

"Exactamundo!" Peaches held open the door for me. "Come in and feast your eyes and tastebuds."

"If it isn't my favorite *signorina*!" a large man in a white apron called from behind one of the shelves. He stuck his head around the corner and I swear he looked exactly like Chef Boyardee on the spaghetti cans. "Peaches! You are looking more beautiful than ever. How's the *bambino*?"

Peaches patted her stomach. "She's starved. That's why we're here. We want to make the feast of the century."

Then Peaches introduced me to her friend, whose name was Giuseppe DeSalvio. "I am most pleased to meet you," he said, flashing a big warm smile at me.

Peaches patted Mr. DeSalvio's arm. "We need the biggest shopping cart you have. Claud and I plan to buy out the store."

And we almost did. It was a tiny shop with tight little aisles. One whole wall was lined with gourmet mustards. Another wall held shelf after shelf of weird exotic foods like (ick!) snails and chocolate-covered grasshoppers and ants.

Peaches didn't miss a single shelf. "I think

we'll need a couple of jars of those calamata olives and definitely a big can of that olive oil. And, Claudia, grab a couple of boxes of angel hair pasta. Have you ever had this anchovy paste on warm Italian bread? It's heaven."

I didn't tell her that anchovies in any form make me want to gag. She was having too much fun. I just nodded and said, "Sounds delicious."

"We'll start the evening with stuffed mushrooms, some country paté, and triple cream Danish blue on little rounds of toast." Peaches didn't stop after she'd covered the shopping list, and she never seemed to look at the prices, either. She just tossed item after item in her cart. We filled the entire grocery cart with all sorts of strange vegetables that she planned to put in the salad, like radicchio and arugula, and lots of items for appetizers. Peaches had decided the main course would be angel hair pasta with a fresh cilantro pesto, loaded with pine nuts and crushed garlic, topped with freshly grated Romano cheese. "It's simple, elegant, and yummy."

I didn't even know what cilantro was. Peaches showed me. It kind of looks like parsley but has bigger leaves. I even tasted a leaf in the store (Mr. DeSalvio offered us tastes of everything). It's really unusual, but I liked it.

After our cart was filled, Peaches clapped

her hands together. "Now for dessert."

"Now you're talking," I said, eyeing the refrigerated display of chocolate tortes, blueberry cheesecakes, and triple layer cakes. "They all look delicious."

"They do." Peaches draped her arm around my shoulder. "Should we cheat and pretend we made the dessert?"

By this time my mouth was practically watering. I nodded vigorously. "I have an idea. Let's eat something here and not even mention dessert."

This made Mr. DeSalvio laugh so hard his stomach bounced up and down, just like Santa's.

"I'm with Claud," Peaches said. "Maybe we should just sample one of those cheesecakes, and we'll take the chocolate torte home with us. How does that sound?"

The cheesecake, smothered in blueberries, was heaven. It practically melted in my mouth. I could hardly wait for dinner.

After we said our farewells to Mr. DeSalvio, we headed for ZuZu's Petals, the flower stand just off Main Street. Peaches bought a huge bouquet of fresh irises for the table. "You can't have an elegant dinner without flowers," she explained to me as we climbed back in the car. Next stop was The Connecticut Yankee Gift Shop. Peaches whipped up to the curb and hopped out of the car, calling over her shoulder, "And candles. We need candlelight."

She was back in just a few minutes. "This dinner is going to be so much fun," Peaches said as she snapped her seat belt in place. "We've got the food, the candles, and flowers. Now all that's left are placecards."

"Placecards?" I repeated. "You mean those little nameplates they put next to your glass at fancy dinners?"

"Exactly." Peaches grinned. "And I know just the person to make them."

"That would be fun," I said, "but how can I do that and help cook dinner?"

"Oh, you don't have to cook," Peaches laughed. "I'll do all of that. I just want you to paint something lovely on each person's card. Do we need to get supplies for that?"

I thought back to the art supplies tucked away in my closet. I'd used up a lot of them working on my sculpture for art class (which still wasn't quite done). "I think probably just some poster board would work," I said. "I have paints. But I do need ink, so that I can use my calligraphy pen for the lettering. They have all that stuff at Art's."

After we circled the block, I hurried into Art's, bought the ink and posterboard, and jumped back in the car. I leaned my head back against the seat. "I feel like we've just done the whirlwind tour of Stoneybrook."

Peaches smiled sideways at me. "We have."

Before we'd left the house, Peaches had written a note for Mom. "Don't lift a finger. We're cooking dinner. P and C." So when we walked in the house, we found Mom, Dad, and Russ, all in the living room, reading the evening paper.

I carried the shopping bags past them into the kitchen while Peaches made a formal announcement. "This evening's meal will be at seven PM. It will be prepared for you by yours truly, assisted by Miss Claudia Kishi. If you will all sit tight, hors d'oeuvres will be served momentarily."

Dad put the paper on the couch beside him and grinned at Mom. "Now *that's* my idea of the perfect house guest!"

Peaches and I raced into the kitchen and, with a loud clanging of pans and slamming of cupboards, we hastily put together the appetizers. Peaches really does make everything fun. She and I sang at least three choruses of "When the moon hits your eye like a big pizza pie, that's *amore!*"

I've always loved the way Peaches treats everything she does like a great adventure. While we worked on dinner, I couldn't help thinking that Mom would never have suggested such a spur-of-the moment project. If Mom was going to make a fancy dinner, she'd spend two weeks carefully planning every detail, several days shopping for supplies, and an entire day just cooking. And she definitely would never suggest we dress up like waiters and draw moustaches on our faces with black eyebrow pencils.

"This will be the final touch," Peaches whispered as we carefully drew little lines under our noses. "I have some bow ties in my bag, and if we each wear one of those with a vest, they'll think they're at Elaine's or some really posh place like that in New York."

At last it was dinnertime. The flowers rested in one of Mom's crystal vases at the center of the table. The placecards, each with a different flower drawn on it, were propped beside blue ceramic plates. Hors d'oeuvres had been served and the candles were now lit. I found a little silver bell in the cupboard and rang it. Then Peaches and I made our appearance. We each had a dish towel draped over one arm.

"Dinner is served!" we announced together.

Mom, Russ, and Dad were tickled, and when they saw the table setting, they couldn't stop saying nice things.

Dinner was delicious and Peaches was the perfect hostess. It's really true what they say about pregnant women. They do have a special glow, and in the soft candlelight Peaches looked absolutely radiant. I couldn't help thinking what a truly special person she was. And I knew for certain that she'd give birth to a truly special baby.

CHAPTER 9

Thursday

I went to Natalie's, prepared to begin the Friendship Campaign. I thought I had it all figured out. But nothing went the way I'd planned it. My big problem was Natalie...

Be Prepared is Shannon Kilbourne's motto. (I think she borrowed it from the Girl Scouts.) At any rate, when she arrived at Natalie's house that afternoon, she was carrying a list of neighbor kids' names and phone numbers, a fully stocked Kid-Kit, and a bag of lemons. She planned to use the list of names to call a few kids, invite them over, and get the ball rolling. (Mrs. Springer had thought it was a wonderful idea.) Shannon's Kid-Kit held some things she hoped would keep a large group of kids busy. And the lemons were for lemonade. Making real lemonade was usually a big hit with her charges.

The second Mrs. Springer left, Shannon turned to Natalie and said, "Okay, Natalie. Today we're going to invite some friends over for you."

"What friends?" Natalie asked.

"The kids in the neighborhood."

"They won't come."

"They might. We'll tell them we're going to play some great games together and then we'll all make lemonade." Shannon marched to the phone and whipped out her list. "I think I'll start with Margo Pike."

"All right." Natalie sighed. "You can try."

The triplets answered the phone. Each one had to say hi to Shannon. Then they passed the phone to Claire, the youngest Pike kid. Finally, Shannon managed to reach Margo.

"Margo? This is Shannon Kilbourne. I'm at Natalie Springer's house."

"Who?" Margo asked.

"Natalie Springer."

"Oh, her."

"Listen, we were going to play some games of Mother, May I and dodge ball, and then squeeze some real lemonade." Shannon hoped her voice sounded excited enough to catch Margo's interest. "Would you like to join us?"

There was a long pause. Finally Margo said, "Who else will be there?"

Shannon was starting to regret that she'd made her phone call in front of Natalie. She didn't want to hurt her feelings.

"Well," she said, in an ultra-cheery voice, "Natalie and I were thinking you could invite some of your friends to come along. Maybe even bring a few of your brothers and sisters over."

"Can I call the Arnold twins?"

"Sure," Shannon said. "The more, the merrier."

"We'll be right over." Margo hung up without saying good-bye.

Shannon put the phone down and smiled broadly at Natalie. "Margo and a few of her friends are coming over. Now all you and I have to do is go outside and wait."

Natalie seemed to be warming to the idea. "Gee, this is almost like having my own party," she said, helping Shannon to carry her Kid-Kit outside. "And if it's my party, I can pick the games we play, can't I?"

"Well, of course." Shannon opened her Kid-Kit and gestured to its contents. "I brought three sets of jacks, a couple of jump ropes, and some colored chalk. If you like, we could play hopscotch till the other kids show up."

"I like hopscotch," Natalie said, bobbing her head up and down. "Let's play that."

Natalie and Shannon drew several bright pastel boxes on the front sidewalk and then looked for good flat stones to toss. Their hopscotch squares attracted the attention of Pamela Harding, who was out on her bike with Leslie Morris and Jannie Gilbert.

"Hi, Natalie," Pamela said as she slowed her bike to a stop on the sidewalk. "Did you draw that?"

Shannon stepped forward. "Yes, and I helped. Do you want to play with us?"

Pamela looked to her friends, who shrugged silently. "Well, maybe just for a little bit." Pamela dropped her bike on its side in the grass, and her friends followed suit.

"I get to go first," Natalie announced, stepping up in front of the hopscotch squares. "Watch!"

Leslie and the others watched as Natalie tossed her rock, made two hops, then tugged at her anklet. When she bent down to pull up her sock, her foot scooted sideways.

"You stepped on the line," Jannie Gilbert cried out.

"Did not," Natalie protested.

Shannon, who had been watching from the other side, could see a pink smear in the line drawn on the sidewalk. "I'm afraid you did, Natalie. Now it's Leslie's turn."

Natalie crossed her arms and shuffled sulkily to the side. Leslie made a perfect run, as did her friends. They were clearly enjoying themselves, giggling when they lost their balance and nearly fell over, cheering for each other when they made it to the finish. Everything would have been fine, except that Natalie wasn't part of their fun at all. It was almost as if she weren't even there.

Maybe the game's the problem, Shannon thought. "I've got an idea," she announced brightly. "Why don't we play dodge ball?"

"But there are only four of us," Natalie pointed out.

"Not any more." Shannon gestured down

the street. The others turned to see Margo and Claire Pike and the Arnold twins rounding the corner. "More recruits!"

Natalie perked up when she saw the new group of kids. "Hurry up!" she shouted. "We're playing dodge ball. I get to throw the ball first."

Shannon was a little surprised by Natalie's "me first" declarations — everything Stacey and I had said about Natalie had made Shannon think she was sweet and shy — but she chalked it up to enthusiasm.

"Everyone line up by my garage," Natalie ordered. "It should be oldest to youngest."

"Why?" Margo asked.

Natalie tucked the ball under her arm and replied bossily, "Because this is my house and I said so."

That set off some definite rumbling in the ranks, but the kids did as they were told. Shannon tapped Natalie on the shoulder and whispered, "I'll go set everything up for the lemonade. Have fun!"

Natalie just nodded. She was too busy preparing her assault on the kids lined up in front of her garage door to talk.

Inside the house, Shannon sliced each lemon in half, and piled the halves in a bowl. She found a plastic pitcher and filled it with water, then carried both the bowl and pitcher out onto the front porch. She'd only been gone about ten minutes, but by the time Shannon returned, everything had changed. The kids were no longer playing dodge ball but facing each other across the yard in two lines, shouting, "Red Rover, Red Rover, send Marilyn right over!"

Natalie was playing, too — she was on the end of one of the lines — but she didn't seem to be very involved. The other kids would laugh and tease each other but none of them ever directed a comment or a joke to her. And no one ever called for Natalie to come over.

"All right, everybody," Shannon called after about fifteen minutes. "It's lemonade time. Who's thirsty?"

"I am!" Carolyn Arnold yelled.

"Me, too," Margo hollered.

"Last one to the porch is a rotten egg," Leslie shouted.

Shannon didn't even have to look to know who would end up as the rotten egg. Natalie climbed the steps last, then shoved her way to the front of the group. "I know how to make lemonade, so I get to squeeze the lemons first."

The kids gave way, but it was very clear to Shannon that they didn't appreciate Natalie's behavior. Shannon let Natalie demonstrate with a few lemons, then said, "Okay, who else wants a turn?"

The children lined up, and each twisted their lemon half on the juicer. After everyone had taken a turn Shannon poured half a cup of sugar into the pitcher and said, "Now it's time to stir. Who would like to do that?"

Shannon wasn't surprised when Natalie stepped forward, but this time she was ready. In a very deliberate tone, Shannon said, "Natalie, why don't you ask one of your friends to stir, and then you can pour the drinks?"

Natalie chose Claire Pike, who took the wooden spoon and swirled the mixture around and around until the sugar had dissolved. Then Natalie took the pitcher around the circle and poured some lemonade into everyone's glasses. She barked orders at the other kids as she went. "Hold your glass up. Don't move. You better not spill. That's enough for you."

With each passing minute Shannon felt more and more miserable. The Friendship Campaign was turning into a complete disaster. She could tell by the sour looks on the children's faces that they probably wouldn't want to play with Natalie again. She was just too bossy.

Shannon was totally wiped out by the experience. That night she called me to talk it over. I was in my usual spot — sitting at my desk, staring at my homework and devouring a bag of pretzels. (I was *trying* to cut out chocolate.)

"The afternoon was a disaster," Shannon moaned. "You should have been there for the big finish. All seven kids chugged their lemonade, tossed their cups in the trash — and left."

"Didn't they say anything?" I asked, digging in the bag for the last of the pretzels.

"Not even good-bye. I think they'd had enough." There was a long pause. Finally Shannon asked, in a tiny voice, "Do you think I blew it, Claud?"

I straightened up in my chair. "First of all, Shannon, you didn't blow it," I said, firmly. "You followed our plans to the letter. You invited some kids over to play with Natalie and you helped set the games in motion. It was up to Natalie to take the ball and run with it."

"Natalie took the ball all right," Shannon said, with a sarcastic snort. "Then she demanded to be first at everything, barked orders at anyone who would listen, and systematically eliminated all possible candidates for future friends."

I chewed thoughtfully on a pretzel. "Boy,

that sure doesn't seem like Natalie. I wonder why she acted that way?"

"I don't know," Shannon replied. "But I think we need a new strategy for the Friendship Campaign."

I poured the remaining crumbs from the pretzel bag into my mouth and murmured, "You're absolutely right about this. We'll bring it up at the next BSC meeting."

Shannon and I chatted for a few more minutes and then a quick glance at my clock made me realize I'd better get back to my homework. "We'll talk more about this tomorrow," I said to Shannon. "In the meantime, I hear the call of a single-celled amoeba."

I hung up the phone and stared at my science book. It was going to be a long night.

CHAPTER 10

Friday. Usually it's the highlight of the week, right? Wrong! I think I had to listen to a lecture from every one of my teachers, including my PE teacher. She thought my sparkle socks were inappropriate for gym class.

Besides, it was really hard to feel excited about the weekend when I knew that a huge stack of homework was lurking on my desk. I knew exactly what I would be doing for the next two days.

For starters, there was the book report I should have done on Tuesday, but Peaches had insisted I help her with that dinner. And I would have completed my sculpture on Wednesday, except that Peaches had asked me to look at baby catalogues with her. She said that I was the only one in the family who had any taste. How could I turn her down? On Thursday, after I'd talked to Shannon, I had been all ready to read those chapters for science, but Peaches had popped in and asked me to help her with her pre-natal exercises. It's really hard to say no to Peaches. She is so fun and, let's face it, homework is so un-fun.

That night I fell into bed completely exhausted. I was anxious to get some sleep and forget all about science and English, sparkly socks, and white sneakers. I had turned out the light and was just drifting off to sleep when I heard the tiniest sound.

Tap. Tap. Tap.

At first I thought it was something scratching against my window. Like a branch. Then I heard it again.

Tap. Tap. Tap.

The sound was definitely coming from inside the house. I lifted myself up on one elbow. Someone was tapping at my door. I squinted at the red numbers on my clock. Eleven-thirty.

"Janine?" I muttered groggily. "Is that you?"

"No, honey," I heard Peaches whisper from the hall. "It's your aunt. Your very hungry aunt."

I flicked on my bedside light and glanced at the empty bag of pretzels still lying on the floor next to my bed. That was the last of my snack supply. "Do you want me to make you a sandwich or something?" I called toward the door.

The door opened a crack. "No. I'm not that kind of hungry." Peaches peered into my room and grinned. "I want a large double cheese, pepperoni, and onion pizza."

I blinked several times. Finally I said, "I don't know how to make that."

Peaches laughed out loud. "I don't expect you to make it. I tried to order it from Pizza-to-Go, but they were just closing up. Pizza Express doesn't deliver after eleven but does stay open till one."

I still didn't see why she had woken me up. "Is Russ going to go pick it up?"

Peaches shook her head. "He's dead asleep. I didn't have the heart to wake him. Besides, I thought you might like to come with me. After all, it *is* Friday night."

Last week she had said, "It *is* Saturday night." Peaches was starting to repeat herself.

"Just think of it," she said, tiptoeing into my room. "Piping hot pizza with lots of bubbling cheese and pepperoni."

"What about anchovies?" I cut in.

"No anchovies." Peaches held up her right hand. "I promise."

Now that I was awake, pizza did sound good. "Will you pay?"

"Of course." Peaches tugged on my arm. "Come on."

"But I'm still in my nightgown."

"That's okay," Peaches said. "Throw on a coat. No one will ever know the difference."

I almost did just that, but a little tiny voice in the back of my brain told me that wasn't such a great idea. What if we were in an accident? I quickly threw on a pair of jeans and a sweater. Everyone in the house was asleep, so Peaches and I held our shoes in our hands until we made it out the front door.

Outside the air was cool and crisp. It was a perfect night for doing something wild and crazy. Peaches and I drove in her car to downtown Stoneybrook. On the way we bellowed a few more off-key choruses of, "When the moon hits your eye like a big pizza pie," at the tops of our lungs. (It was turning into our theme song.)

Pizza Express was packed with high school kids. We grabbed a table near the back corner. Then Peaches put two dollars in the juke box and told me to pick anything I wanted to hear. She ordered us a large combo deluxe pizza pie, with a side of bread sticks and marinara sauce. Then she got a soda for me and a huge chocolate milkshake for herself.

"I feel like a kid again," Peaches said as she happily slurped her milkshake.

I pointed out kids I recognized from Janine's class and we made up scenarios about their lives. Then we pretended to be a dating service and paired the most unlikely kids together. Peaches and I laughed so hard that tears were streaming down our cheeks.

An hour and a half zoomed by, and before we knew it Pizza Express was closing. A guy in a white shirt and apron was stacking chairs on top of tables, while a girl was busy mopping the floor behind the counter. I looked around at the empty restaurant and got the weirdest feeling.

"Peaches?" I asked as we slipped on our jackets. "Did you leave a note for Mom?"

Peaches frowned. "Oops. I meant to, but I guess I forgot."

Downtown Stoneybrook was as deserted as the restaurant. Only a few cars were parked on the street, and most of the storefronts were dark. Everything looked kind of ominous. "I hope we don't get in trouble," I muttered.

Peaches looped her arm through mine. "You worry too much. I'm sure your mom and dad are still snoring happily away in their room. They'll never even know we were gone."

"I hope you're right." But I had a sinking feeling that she was going to be wrong.

Peaches tried to make conversation on the way home, but I was too worried to talk. Mom hadn't been very pleased with me lately. My grades were down and she knew perfectly well about all the homework that had been going untouched night after night. She was only giving me a break because Peaches was visiting.

I was holding my breath when we turned the corner onto Bradford Court, but I quickly let it out in dismay. "Oh, no!"

The windows in my house were ablaze with light.

"I bet they're all up," I said, slumping down in the seat.

Peaches checked her watch. "It's barely after one," she said. "That's not too late. After all, it *is* Friday night."

"I wish you'd quit saying that," I grumbled as Peaches parked the car.

Mom met us at the front door in her robe and nightgown. "Where have you been?" she demanded in a tight voice. "You scared me half to death."

"I'm sorry, Mom," I murmured. "We should have left a note."

Mom made both of us sit on the couch. Then she paced back and forth, ranting and raving. I've never seen her so worked up. And I felt as though all of her anger were directed at me.

"What was going through your head, Claudia? I got up to get a drink of water, walked by your room, and found the door open and you missing. I didn't know what had happened. I was worried sick."

"I said I was sorry." I stared at my hands clasped tightly in my lap and felt the warmth rising to my cheeks. I really hate being scolded. But when it happens in front of people it's too embarrassing for words.

Finally, Peaches spoke up. "Look, Rioko, I've very sorry. This is all my fault. I was hungry, so I woke Claud up and asked her to go for a pizza with me."

"A *pizza*!" Mom threw her hands in the air. "There's plenty of food in the house. If you were so hungry, why didn't you just make a sandwich here?"

I could tell Peaches was feeling just as uncomfortable about being yelled at as I was. She shrugged and murmured, "I had a craving."

Mom did a silent stroll back and forth in front of us. I think she was recharging her battery because she started in again. "I'm not going to punish you, Claudia, because you were with an adult — " She narrowed her eyes at Peaches as she said the word. "An adult who should have known better. But I am most definitely not happy with your behavior."

"I promise I won't do it again," was all I could say. My face was getting warmer by the minute and I could feel tears of embarrassment and frustration threatening to overflow any second.

"I'm just so disappointed in you, Claudia," Mom went on. "We have been very lenient with you about your homework lately. Meanwhile your grades keep getting worse and worse. And midnight excursions like this don't help matters one bit."

That was it. I couldn't sit there another minute and listen to my mother accuse me of deliberately avoiding my homework.

"It's *not* my fault," I shouted. "I try to do my homework, but every time I open a book Peaches is there wanting me to help cook a big dinner, or look at some catalogues, or help with her exercises. I mean, what am I supposed to do?" I pointed to Peaches. "If you want to yell at somebody — yell at her. She's *your* sister!"

Everything was a blur as I turned and raced up to my room. I think Peaches may have called after me, but I didn't want to hear her. I slammed the door and threw myself onto my bed.

CHAPTER 11

The weekend seemed endless. I felt rotten and Peaches looked miserable. I didn't mean to ignore her, but I really didn't know what to say to her. So I spent a lot of time in my room.

Finally at lunch on Sunday Peaches asked if I would like to work with her on planning the baby's room. "You could help me pick out fabric for the curtains and wallpaper, and maybe we can even find a frieze for the wall. I've brought a whole stack of swatch books home from the store."

I knew it was Peaches' way of trying to make peace, so I couldn't say no. "Sure," I said. "I think I'd really like that. But I can't do it today. I have to finish my homework."

Peaches pursed her lips. "I understand, Claudia," she said, giving my mom a sideways glance. "Your homework should come first."

"Maybe we could look at your books tomorrow after school," I replied politely.

"Tomorrow would be fine."

We sounded so formal. It made me cringe inside, but I didn't know how else to act. It was clear that something had come between us, and we were fumbling for a way to move past it. I took a bite of my sandwich and hoped that maybe this was just an awkward phase we had to work through.

I worked all Sunday afternoon and evening on my school work, and I still didn't finish everything. When you fall behind, it's really hard to catch up. I didn't want to listen, but this tiny voice inside my head kept saying, "It's all Peaches' fault." So instead of growing less angry, the more I worked, the more resentful I felt.

"Do you need any help with your work, Claudia?" Peaches asked when I came down to the kitchen for a snack that evening.

"What do you know about anemones?" I shot back a little grumpily.

Peaches winced. "Not much. I think they're pink."

I opened the refrigrator without even looking at her. "Then I guess you can't help me."

Peaches left the kitchen without another word. As I poured myself a glass of milk and grabbed a handful of cookies, I felt bad that

I'd been so rude. But then that tiny voice said, "She promised to help before and never came through. Now she offers, but she doesn't know anything about science. She's a wash-out."

I didn't see Peaches again until after school on Monday. I'd forgotten all about our plan to look at wallpaper books. Instead I was hoping to work on my sculpture. I'd salvaged a whole box of Styrofoam peanuts from the Dumpster at school — I thought they would add wonderful texture to my piece. So let's just say I was less than enthusiastic when Peaches met me at the front door.

"Hi, Claud," she called cheerily. "I have the swatch books all laid out on the coffee table. I even fixed us a snack to eat while we think."

My shoulders slumped. "Oh, the wallpaper. I forgot about it."

Peaches pursed her lips. "If it isn't convenient, I can take a rain check."

"No." I sighed. "There'll never be a convenient time. Let's just get it over with."

"Get it over with?" Peaches clipped each word as she spoke. "If that's how you feel about it, then forget it. I don't want you to help me."

I really hadn't intended to make her angry, so I quickly tried to change what I'd said. "I didn't mean that the way it sounded," I tried to explain. "It's just that I'm feeling a little overloaded — "

"Look, Claudia," Peaches cut in. "I'm sorry that my presence here is complicating your life. But you're not the only one who has problems, you know. Russ and I are trying to deal with moving *and* having a baby *and* buying a new house. And I'm trying to deal with quitting my job. It doesn't help matters to have to deal with a sulky teenager. I said I was sorry about taking you out for pizza, so would you *please* just get over it!"

With that, Peaches turned and marched into the den. I was left speechless.

Just then the doorbell rang. It was Mary Anne, ready for our next knitting lesson. I'd forgotten about that, too.

"Claudia, what's the matter?" Mary Anne asked when I opened the front door. "You look like you've just seen a ghost."

I put my finger to my lips and gestured for Mary Anne to follow me upstairs. I was afraid Peaches might overhear our conversation. When we reached my room I said, "I don't think I want to work on the blanket anymore. I'll give you back your yarn. Maybe you can do something else with it."

"Did something happen with your aunt again?" Mary Anne asked. Of course I had told my friends about my frustrations with Peaches and how my mom had yelled at me on Friday. They were sympathetic, but encouraged me to work it out. "I thought you were going to try to smooth things over."

"I know, I know." I flopped miserably onto my bed. "But I was grumpy with her when I came home from school, and Peaches really let me have it."

I tried to relay the exact words that had passed between us. Mary Anne listened carefully until I was through. "It sounds like you're both on edge," she said. "I'm sure Peaches didn't want to hurt your feelings. And you didn't want to hurt hers, did you?"

"No." My lip was quivering a little. "I love Peaches. It's just that she can be so pushy."

"But isn't that also one of the things you like about her?" Mary Anne asked gently. "I mean, if she weren't pushy, you guys would never have had half the adventures you've had."

Mary Anne was right. But it was hard for me to admit it.

"Don't stop working on the blanket just because of this little spat," Mary Anne continued. "After all, nothing so very terrible has happened. You've both said a few things that you probably wish you hadn't. That's all. You'll make up soon and everything will be fine. And besides, the present is for the baby, right? And you're not mad at the baby, are you?"

"Of course not," I murmured.

"Well, then you better keep knitting. Because . . ." Mary Anne grinned. "At the rate you're going, the baby will be twelve before the blanket's done."

"Oh, all right." I dug the yarn out of my closet and handed it to Mary Anne. Mary Anne held up the inch-long blanket and raised an eyebrow.

"I know, I know," I muttered. "I haven't done a stitch all week."

"Well, the good news is," she said diplomatically, "you haven't made any more mistakes."

That made me giggle. It was the first laugh I'd had in at least three days, and it felt good. As our lesson progressed, I felt better and better. By the time the Monday afternoon BSC meeting started, I was actually feeling cheery.

Kristy called the meeting to order and then Shannon reported on the Friendship Campaign.

"I hate to admit it," Shannon began, "but Plan A didn't work. I invited some kids to come play with Natalie, but all they did was cluster into their own groups. None of them wanted to play with her. And frankly, I don't blame them. She turned into a really bossy, unpleasant little girl."

"Natalie's really a very sweet kid," I said. "Odd, maybe, but not bratty. I think we should give this campaign another chance."

"Claud's right," Stacey said. "Maybe Natalie wasn't feeling well that day or something."

Kristy tugged at her visor. "You know what? It sounds like the kids she already knows fell into the old pattern of ignoring Natalie. And she was uncomfortable, so she acted bossy. Maybe it's time to introduce her to a whole new batch of kids — ones she's never met before — and let her make a fresh start."

"I'm supposed to sit for Natalie on Wednesday," Jessi said, checking the schedule in her dance bag. "Why don't I take her to my neighborhood? I'll ask Becca to introduce Natalie to her friends."

"Great," Kristy said. "On with Plan B!"

The rest of the meeting was really busy. Everybody left in a good mood, and I was reasonably happy, too. But as I waved goodbye from the open door, I caught sight of Peaches' stack of wallpaper books, and my warm glow evaporated. Despite my talk with Mary Anne, I really didn't feel any differently about Peaches. It was hard to forget her harsh words.

CHAPTER 12

Wednesday

You guys, I'm really glad we had that discussion on Monday. I have to admit, after listening to your story, Shannon, I was a little nervous about this job, but things worked out great. The fresh start idea was terrific.

Jessi's first meeting with Natalie started pretty much the way everyone else's had. Not long after Mrs. Springer left, Natalie turned to Jessi and said, "Will you be my friend?"

"I'll be your friend, Natalie," Jessi answered, taking Natalie firmly by the hand. "And I'll also introduce you to some of my friends."

"Your friends? Are they here?"

"Nope. I'm going to take you to meet them. But first I need to write your mom a note."

Jessi told Mrs. Springer where they were headed, in case Mrs. Springer came home earlier than expected. And Jessi left a phone number where they could be reached. She taped the note to the refrigerator, where Mrs. Springer couldn't miss it.

"Come on," Jessi said, turning to Natalie and rubbing her hands together. "Let's go meet some kids."

"What kids?" Natalie asked warily.

"My sister and some of her friends," Jessi replied.

They walked hand in hand the few blocks to Jessi's house. When they arrived, Becca and Charlotte Johanssen were playing jump rope in the front yard. One end of the rope was tied to a tree and Charlotte was twirling the other end.

"Not last night but the night before," Becca chanted as she jumped, "twenty-four robbers came knocking at my door. I ran out and they ran in, hit them over the head with a rolling pin."

"Hi, Becca. Hi, Char," Jessi called. "Say hi to Natalie!"

Becca didn't stop jumping. She just called, in rhythm with the rope, "Nice to meet you, Nat-a-lie!"

Natalie, who was still holding on to Jessi's hand, suddenly became incredibly shy. She ducked behind Jessi and murmured, "Hello," so softly that only Jessi heard her.

Jessi had made a few calls on Tuesday, inviting kids to come to her house after school. For half a second she was afraid they weren't going to show up. But they soon began arriving from all directions. First the Hobart boys showed up. James, who's eight, was towing his four-year-old brother, Johnny, in a red wagon. Mathew, who's six, carried a soccer ball under one arm.

"G'day, Jessi," James called (the Hobarts have these great Australian accents). "Is this the girl we're supposed to meet?"

Jessi stepped sideways and gestured to Natalie, who couldn't stop staring at James. "Yep. This is Natalie. And Natalie, meet the Hobarts. They're from Down Under."

"Down under?" Natlie shoved her glasses up on her nose, totally confused.

"She means we're from Australia," James explained.

"Wow, that's a long way away." Natalie was impressed.

Mathew tossed the ball in the air. "Halfway around the world."

There was a long pause as the Hobart boys and Natalie stared at each other. Finally Mathew held up the ball and asked, "Who wants to play kickball?"

"I do!"

The answer came from half a block away. Jessi spotted a girl with a thick halo of red hair skipping down the sidewalk. "Hi, Rosie!" she called. "Come and meet Natalie."

Rosie Wilder is really talented and outgoing. She's one of my favorite kids to baby-sit for. She saw Jessi and did a grand *jeté* (that's a leap that looks like a split — I know that much from hanging around Jessi), then landed in a curtsy in front of Natalie. "Hi, I'm Rosie."

Natalie smiled and took several steps backward. She backed up so far that she tripped over Johnny's wagon and fell flat on her seat.

"That's what I call being bowled over," Jessi joked. "Rosie always has that effect on people."

Rosie giggled, but Natalie blushed. And not just her cheeks — her whole face went bright pink.

Luckily James shouted, "Rosie, step on it, will you? We want to play ball!"

Rosie raced to join them and nearly collided with Jamie Newton, who was running from the opposite direction, accompanied by Mary Anne. He scooped up the kickball and shouted, "I'm the first pitcher!"

"No fair!" Mathew shouted. "We were here first, so we get to pitch first."

The game of kickball quickly turned into a game of keepaway as the kids chased Jamie all over the yard trying to grab the ball.

"Go and play with them," Jessi urged Natalie. "It looks like they're having fun."

"They don't want to play with me. They don't even know me."

Jessi had braced herself for heading off some bossiness, but Natalie was acting anything but bossy. In fact, she was being so clingy that Jessi was starting to feel concerned. She was about to coax Natalie into joining the kickball game one more time, when she noticed that Natalie wasn't watching the game at all. Her attention was focused on Becca and Charlotte and the jump rope.

"Do you know how to jump rope?" Jessi asked Natalie.

Natalie nodded firmly. "I know some good jumping rhymes, too."

"Great! Why don't you teach them to Becca and Charlotte?"

"I couldn't," Natalie said, backing away once more. "They probably already know them, anyway."

"Let's go see." Jessi took Natalie by the hand and they approached the girls.

"Becca?" Jessi called. "Natalie says she knows some pretty good jump rope rhymes. Would you two like to learn them?"

Charlotte, who was jumping, stopped immediately. The rope dropped around her ankles. "Sure. I'm really tired of 'Not last night but the night before.' We've done it at least twenty times."

Natalie clasped her hands in front of her and stared at the toes of her shoes. "Do you guys know Teddy Bear, Teddy Bear?"

Becca and Charlotte looked at each other and shrugged. "No."

"How about One Frog, Two Frog?" Natalie asked.

They didn't know that one either.

"That's my favorite," Natalie said, lifting her chin and smiling a little. "Because at one part you have to jump like a frog."

"That sounds fun," Becca said. "Why don't you show us?"

Natalie looked to Jessi for support. "Go ahead, Natalie," Jessi said. "Show them. And don't worry if you mess up."

"Yeah," Becca added. "I've stepped on the rope five times today."

"Six," Charlotte corrected her.

"Okay, six," Becca said with a grin. She untied the rope from the tree, adding, "I'm glad you want to play with us, Natalie. Sometimes it's hard to jump with the rope tied to the tree."

Charlotte nodded. "It catches on the bark and then we have to start all over."

Once they had untied the rope from the tree, the girls moved over to the driveway, where it would be easier to jump. Charlotte and Becca stood ready to twirl. Natalie took a deep breath and said, "I'll start with Teddy Bear, Teddy Bear, because that's the easiest. I hope I don't forget it."

"You won't," Jessi said. "Just get in there and jump."

The rope looped high in the air several times. Finally Natalie got up her nerve, ran into the middle, and began to chant her jump rope rhyme.

"Teddy Bear, Teddy Bear, turn around;
Teddy Bear, Teddy Bear, touch the ground.
Teddy Bear, Teddy Bear, run upstairs;

Teddy Bear, Teddy Bear, say your prayers.
Teddy Bear, Teddy Bear, turn out the light;
Teddy Bear, Teddy Bear, say goodnight."

Jessi watched as Becca and Charlotte each took a turn at Teddy Bear, Teddy Bear. Then Natalie showed them One Frog, Two Frog. She had to help them with the words and motions, but she never sounded bossy. And when she stepped on the rope she wasn't embarrassed at all. In fact, Natalie, who had started out so shy, now wore a grin that stretched from ear to ear.

Jessi pumped her fist in the air. "Yes! Plan B is off and running!"

CHAPTER 13

J essi broke the good news about the Natalie Friendship Campaign at the next BSC meeting. All of us congratulated her. It was my turn to sit for Natalie on Saturday and I must say, I was totally amazed. She never once asked me about being her friend. (Normally she would have mentioned it *at least* four times.)

In fact, after Natalie had finished the celery-and-peanut butter snack her mom had left for her, she carried her plate to the sink and asked, "Is it all right if I invite Becca and Charlotte to come over and play?"

"Yes, of course." I was delighted.

"Let's call them right now." Natalie ran to find the phone book. "Would you help me look up their numbers?"

I was glad that the Friendship Campaign was going so well. And I wanted to make sure it would be a long term success. Suddenly, I had an idea. "I'll look up the phone numbers,"

I said, "but first you and I need to have a talk."

"About what?" Natalie asked.

"About friendship." I took Natalie by the hand and led her to the couch in the living room. I found some brightly colored construction paper in my Kid-Kit, and spread it out on the coffee table. "I think we should write down the rules of friendship."

"You mean, like the Ten Commandments?" Natalie asked, wide-eyed.

"Sort of," I said, holding back a giggle. "But we'll make up these rules ourselves."

"Oh, I like that." Natalie reached for one of the colored markers in my Kid-Kit. "How do we start?"

"Well, first let's write on our paper, 'A good friend is,' " I suggested. "Then we'll fill in the blank."

"Okay." Natalie squinched one eye shut and concentrated on her lettering. As she wrote she spoke the words out loud. "A good friend is . . . nice."

"Good rule!" I said. "Now it's my turn. A good friend knows how to share." I wrote my rule neatly below Natalie's entry.

"That's really important," Natalie said, looking down at my sentence. "I know some kids who never share their toys."

"There are all kinds of ways to share. Isn't

taking turns sharing?" I asked Natalie. "And letting someone else go first, or letting someone else be captain?"

"Oh. Yes." Natalie was probably thinking very hard about her afternoon with Shannon, when she had insisted on being first and the boss of every game they played. She bent over the paper and printed, "A good friend is never bossy."

"That's a great one, Natalie." I patted her on the shoulder. "It's easy to be bossy, isn't it?"

Natalie nodded. "Sometimes I've been kind of bossy."

"Really?" I tried to act surprised.

"But I'm not going to be that way anymore," she added.

"Maybe we should add to our list that a good friend listens to other kids."

"You mean, like when they want to play something that you don't?" Natalie asked, cocking her head.

"Yes. A good friend would listen to her friends' suggestions and maybe take turns, playing their game first before her own."

"That way everybody wins!" Natalie said. "How do you spell 'listens'?"

I told her (or tried to), and then while she wrote, I studied our list, thinking about my friends and what I like about them. "My friend

120

Mary Anne is really good at being kind and saying nice things, even when her own feelings are hurt."

"Did you ever get your feelings hurt?" Natalie asked.

I nodded sadly, thinking about Peaches. "And then I've said things that I wish I hadn't. It only made me feel worse."

"Me, too," Natalie said. "I'm going to write, 'a good friend never calls people names, or hurts their feelings.' And underline it."

"That's worth underlining twice," I said, reaching for a bright red marker.

While I was adding another line, I decided to write, *a good friend admits when she's made a mistake.*

"And a good friend says she's sorry," Natalie added.

"That's right," I murmured. "And she lets bygones be bygones."

We drew decorations around the edges of the page. I chose fish and seahorses. Natalie made spirals and sunflowers. Then we tacked our completed list of friendship rules on the bulletin board in the Springers' kitchen. Here's what it said:

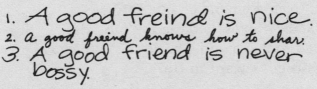

1. A good freind is nice.
2. a good freind knows how to shar.
3. A good friend is never bossy.

4. A good freind lissens to her friends and takes turns.
5. <u>A good freind never calls peeple names, or hurts their felings.</u>
6. a good freind admits when she's made a misstake.
7. a good freind says I'm sory and means it.

Natalie and I proudly read our rules out loud. Then I gave her a big hug and said, "Come on. Let's go call Becca and Char."

About ten minutes later, Becca and Charlotte were cutting across the neighbor's lawn with jump rope in hand.

"Ready to jump rope?" Becca called.

"I'm all set," Natalie replied as she raced out to join them in the driveway. The three girls quickly settled the question of who would turn the rope and who would jump. Then they tried to pick a chant.

"I want to do Fudge, Fudge, Call the Judge," Natalie announced firmly.

All I had to do was clear my throat, and say, "Nat? Remember our list?"

Natalie's eyes widened. "Oh, right." She turned to Becca and Charlotte. "Which rhyme do you guys want to do?"

They took a vote. First they'd do Teddy Bear, Teddy Bear and *then* they'd do Fudge, Fudge, Call the Judge.

After Natalie got past that awkward moment, I didn't have to do anything. I sat on the front steps with my sketch pad and watched the girls have fun. Natalie did step on the rope once and deny it, but a quick glance in my direction reminded her of our sixth rule — a good friend admits her mistakes. Quickly, she said, "Maybe I *did* step on the rope after all. Sorry, you guys."

I was pretty proud of Natalie. And Charlotte and Becca seemed to be viewing her differently, too. As they were leaving Charlotte asked, "Is it all right if we come back Monday?"

"Sure," Natalie said. "And maybe next week I can check out this book of jump roping rhymes from my school library."

"Someone wrote a book about jump rope chants?" Becca asked.

"Yeah," Natalie said, tugging at her saggy sock. "It's called, *Easy, Ivy, Overs.*"

"I hope you can find it," Charlotte said enthusiastically. "It would be fun to read."

"I'll go to the library first thing Monday morning," Natalie replied. "That way we'll be sure to have it that afternoon."

"See ya, Nat!" Becca and Charlotte sang in

unison as they skipped down the street.

"See you guys!" Natalie waved until they were out of sight. Then she turned to me and sighed, "That was one of the best days I ever had."

"It's nice to have friends, isn't it?" I said, draping my arm around her shoulder and walking her back to the house.

"It sure is."

After Mrs. Springer returned, I shuffled through the leaves back to my house. On the way home, I did a lot of thinking. About friends. And about Peaches. I realized how much her friendship meant to me.

I kicked at a pile of leaves and thought, "I could have just said no when she asked me to do things. I didn't have to shout at her."

I had just been frustrated about school and I'd dumped all of my anger on her. I realized that I had not been nice (rule #1 on the list) and I had hurt her feelings (rule #5).

An apology was definitely in order (rule #7). I resolved to find Peaches and tell her how sorry I was the minute I got home.

CHAPTER 14

Remember that tingly feeling I had before Peaches' first phone call? The one that told me something was going to happen? Well, I felt it again, as I walked up the steps to my house. Only this time it didn't feel so good.

"Hey! Where is everybody?" I called as I opened the front door. The Volvo wasn't in the driveway. Both cars were gone from the garage, and there were hardly any lights on in the house. "Peaches? Mom? Anybody?" I shouted.

I heard a loud sniff from the kitchen, so I headed that way. The tiny light shone from above the stove. A figure was sitting in the half darkness with her hand on the phone.

"Janine?" A knot had formed in my stomach and it was getting tighter by the second. "Is something wrong?"

Janine raised her head to look at me. I could

see a tear stain on her cheek. "Oh, Claudia! It's so sad."

"What?" I practically shouted. "Tell me. What's sad?"

"Peaches lost the baby."

"Oh, no!" I gasped. "When did it happen? How?"

"Peaches was all by herself this afternoon when she started to feel bad. She knew something was wrong, so she called Russ. He got here at the same time that I did and rushed Peaches to the hospital."

"Do Mom and Dad know?"

Janine nodded. "They'd gone out to lunch but I phoned them at the restaurant and they hurried over to meet Peaches and Russ at the hospital." She gestured to the phone and added, "Mom just called and told me the news."

"Poor Peaches." My eyes started to burn with tears. "And poor Russ."

"They wanted this baby so badly." Janine said, almost to herself. "I don't know what went wrong."

Suddenly I had this really terrible thought. I had been rotten to Peaches, and she had been seriously upset with me. What if all of that emotional turmoil had made her have a miscarriage? Then it would be my fault. I slumped down in a chair and put my head in my hands.

"Oh, no. Oh, this is just too awful."

Janine and I sat in the darkness for at least an hour. Mostly we were quiet. Now and then we talked a little, about how unfair life could be. My insides ached. I wanted to tell Janine my fear — that I might have been responsible for the miscarriage — but the thought was too awful to even say out loud.

Finally Mom and Dad came home. When Janine and I heard their car turn into the driveway, we hurried to the front door. "Is Peaches all right?" I asked, fearing the worst.

Mom nodded grimly. "She's out of danger, but the doctors decided to keep her at the hospital overnight for observation. Russ feels certain that she'll be able to come home tomorrow."

"How's he handling this?" Janine asked.

"Russ is coping," Dad replied. "Of course, he's sad about the baby, but mostly he's worried about Peaches. So he's staying with her until visiting hours are over."

"Do they know why this happened?" I asked in a tiny voice.

Mom shook her head. "We'll know more later."

I wanted to confess to Mom that *I* knew what had happened, but I didn't have the courage. Instead I sat in the living room with everyone else. The silence was horrible. No one knew what to do or say. Mom and Dad didn't even take off their coats but just sat there, thinking. Every now and then Mom would murmur, "I suppose I should make some dinner." Then Dad or Janine would say, "I'm really not very hungry." And no one would move.

Finally Russ came home, looking pretty tired. His eyes were red and puffy, which meant he had probably been crying. When he saw us sitting there, he said, "I think you could use some good news."

"Do you have any?" I managed to ask.

Russ took off his coat and held it in his lap as he sat on the arm of the couch. "The doctors say that Peaches is absolutely fine, and that this . . . this was just one of those things. They feel certain that we can try again." Russ stared at his coat. "Though I think we may wait quite awhile."

Mom and Dad looked at him and murmured, "We understand."

I still had that knot in my stomach. I knew it wouldn't go away until I talked to Peaches. The night was long and bleak. Russ was too restless to sleep. Somewhere around eleven o'clock he put his coat on and drove back to the hospital. "I just want to be there if Peaches wakes up," I heard him explain to Mom.

I tried to sleep, but tossed and turned all

night. The awful things I'd said to Peaches echoed over and over again in my head. And I couldn't stop thinking about the baby.

Late Sunday morning Russ brought Peaches back from the hospital. Mom met her at the front door. They didn't say much, but held each other tight. Dad told Peaches how sorry we all were, and she nodded that she understood. Janine and I stood in the background waiting for a chance to say something.

"I think you ought to rest now," Russ said to Peaches, ushering her toward the den.

"Yes, of course," Mom said. "We'll get out of your way."

"If you need anything," Dad said, "just — "

"I know," Peaches cut in. She looked at us and smiled weakly. "Thanks, everybody. Don't worry, I'm all right."

And then they went into the den.

We all went through the motions of acting like everything was normal but, of course, it wasn't. Mom and Janine went into the kitchen to make lunch, and Dad took Russ to the drugstore to have a prescription filled. I knew Peaches was resting and I shouldn't disturb her, but I didn't know when I'd have another chance to talk to her alone. I tiptoed toward the den and peered inside.

Peaches was lying on her side on the couch, hugging a pillow in her arms. Russ had tucked a blue-and-green afghan around her legs. I saw that her eyes were closed and I started to move away, but I must have made a noise because she opened them and smiled.

"Hi, Claud," she said.

"Hi."

My voice cracked and Peaches sat up gingerly. "Claudia, are you okay?"

I couldn't hold it in any longer. The words tumbled out of my mouth in a rush.

"Oh, Peaches, I am so sorry! It was all my fault."

"What are you talking about?"

"If I hadn't been so selfish and terrible, you never would have gotten upset." I threw myself into Peaches' arms and sobbed. "I know I made you lose the baby. I'd do anything to take it all back."

Peaches wrapped her arms around me and held me tight. For a long time we just cried about the lost baby. About our friendship. About everything.

"Oh, Claudia, my Claudia," Peaches murmured as she stroked my hair. I closed my eyes. She sounded and felt like Mimi. Sweet, comforting Mimi. "You must understand. This wasn't your fault. It was nobody's fault."

"It wasn't?" I asked, still holding tight.

"No. It was nature's way of saying that something was wrong. Even though it doesn't seem that way now, it was probably for the best."

Her voice caught a little when she said those words, and I realized that Peaches was trying to convince herself that they were true.

I sat up and rubbed my eyes. "Before all of this happened, I was going to apologize to you — "

"You don't need to apologize," Peaches cut in.

"Yes, I do," I said, firmly. "You see, I realized how important your friendship was to me and that I hadn't been acting like a very good friend. In fact, you were right when you called me a sulky teenager."

"Oh, Claudia, I only said that in anger."

"I know, but you were right to be angry. Wait here."

I gestured for Peaches to stay seated on the couch. I ran to my room, taking the stairs two at a time. I opened the door to my closet. There in the corner was the baby blanket.

"See?" I said, bursting back into the den a minute later. I held up the knitting needles, with the two inches of lavender blanket still attached. "I was knitting this for the baby. I worked on it even after our fight, so how angry could I have been?"

"Let me see that," Peaches said softly.

I handed Peaches my knitting project. It

hardly looked like a blanket. More like a skinny scarf.

"Mary Anne has been teaching me," I explained. "And . . . well . . . Mimi taught Mary Anne."

Peaches took the needles and yarn and hugged them gently to her chest. Then she looked at me with moist eyes. "Mimi would be very proud of you."

I nodded, feeling a giant lump forming in my throat. "I'm going to keep working on this blanket. When it's finished, it will be for the next baby."

When I said "next baby," Peaches wrapped her arms around me again. "Thank you, Claudia," she said, barely choking out the words. "I hope there will be another baby."

"There will," I said through my tears. "I just know it."

CHAPTER 15

Our month with Russ and Peaches came to an end that next Saturday, the day they moved into their new house. Bohren's Movers transported all of the furniture they'd had in storage, but we helped move everything else.

It looked like a parade, with both of our cars following Russ as he drove slowly over to their new home in his station wagon, once again loaded down with boxes and pillows.

Janine and I rode in the back seat of Mom's car, clutching baskets filled with fruit and food supplies.

"Their house looks like something out of *Better Homes and Gardens*," Janine commented as Mom pulled into the driveway. "I mean, look! A perfect Cape-Cod-style house with a white picket fence, big backyard with a climbing tree and huge front porch. All they need is a dog and — "

Janine paused and I finished the sentence for her. "Kids."

She smiled weakly at me. "Yes, kids."

It was really sad, looking up at their perfect family home. They had bought it with the baby in mind, and now there was no baby. Mom had canceled the order from Baby and Company, so the nursery would sit empty. At least for now.

Peaches led us on a tour of the house, pausing every few minutes to call more instructions to the movers. "Put the big bed in the master bedroom upstairs. And the sleeper couch goes in the room next to it," she said as we inched past a man in green overalls struggling to carry a large mattress up the stairs.

"I like a house with light," Peaches said, gesturing to the tall windows. "And this one has plenty."

She opened the door to the room next to the master bedroom. We peered inside at a bright corner room with gleaming hardwood floors.

"The guest room will serve as my study," she explained. "I talked to my office and they said they could offer me plenty of freelance work to do at home."

"Oh, Peaches, that's perfect," Mom said, giving her a quick squeeze. "And just what you wanted."

134

"That way, if we have a baby, I can still continue to work part-time from here." Peaches gestured to the nursery with a wan smile. "This room looks pretty empty right now, but Russ and I have agreed to start thinking about trying again."

I crossed my fingers when she said that and made a secret wish that it would happen soon.

We celebrated the move into their *Father Knows Best* house (as Russ called it) with a backyard barbecue. Barbecues are usually reserved for summer, but Russ and Peaches insisted we eat outside in the brisk autumn air. (I was glad to see that they'd returned to their kooky ways.) Peaches dug into one of the wardrobe boxes and found funny hats and scarves for all of us. Then Dad brought over our hibachi and we made shish kebabs. Russ even managed to pull out the lawn furniture the movers had stacked in the garage, and all of us watched the sun disappear behind the big golden maple trees that lined their back fence.

On Sunday I called Stacey and asked her to come over. We sat on my bed eating carrots (hers) and chocolate stars (mine), marveling at all that had happened during the last four weeks.

"It's hard to believe that Peaches and Russ lived with us for a whole month," I said. "It really only felt like a week or two."

"You guys sure did a lot," Stacey said. "I mean, you went on a gigantic shopping spree at Baby and Company, had a late night adventure at Pizza Express — "

"I met Mr. DeSalvio and discovered In Good Taste," I continued. "Plus I saw some wonderful old movies, and even learned to knit."

"When are you going to show me your blanket?" Stacey asked. "I'm dying to see it."

I had been hesitant to show the blanket to anyone but Mary Anne and Peaches before it was completely finished. But I had made some headway during the past week, and it was actually starting to look like a real blanket. I brought it out of my closet and held it up for Stacey to see.

"What do you think?" I asked, hiding my face behind it.

"Oh, Claud, it's great," Stacey cried. "I didn't know it was going to have that block pattern in it. That must be really hard to do."

"No, not really," I said with a shrug. "You just knit five, purl five, and then reverse it in the next row." As I spoke I looked over at Mimi's portrait and grinned. She *would* have been proud of me!

"Well, as long as we're doing show and tell," Stacey said, hopping off the bed, "I want you to come to my house and see the new hat my dad sent from New York. It's velvet, with all these patches of different colors, and it has this really cool bead work around the brim."

"It sounds so cool."

We walked over to Stacey's, passing Natalie Springer's house on the way. Charlotte, Becca, and Natalie were in the driveway playing — what else? — jumprope.

"Those three have practically become inseparable," I commented as Stacey and I paused to watch them. "All they do is jump rope."

"And sing those darn rhymes." Stacey tossed her head from side to side and chanted, "Fudge Fudge. Call the Judge. Momma's gotta a newborn baby. It ain't no boy. It ain't no girl. It's just an ordinary baby."

Just then Charlotte shouted, "Wait a minute, Natalie. You have to share, remember? That's rule number two."

"Oh, sorry, Char," Natalie said. "I guess I forgot." Then she called in my direction, "Rule number six."

I smiled at Stacey and explained, "Rule number six is, a good friend admits when she's wrong."

We waved good-bye to the jump ropers and continued down the street. "You know," I said, looping my arm through Stacey's, "I thought this past month was hard, but some really good things came out of it."

"That's right. Our Friendship Campaign was a big success."

"And Peaches and Russ moved back to Stoneybrook, so now we can see them as often as we like."

Just mentioning Peaches' name made a lump form in my throat. Stacey squeezed my arm. "Now that they're settled in their new home, maybe they will be able to have a baby."

"I hope so," I whispered to Stacey. "I truly hope so."

About the Author

ANN M. MARTIN did *a lot* of baby-sitting when she was growing up in Princeton, New Jersey. She is a former editor of books for children, and was graduated from Smith College.

Ms. Martin lives in New York City with her cats, Mouse and Rosie. She likes ice cream and *I Love Lucy*; and she hates to cook.

Ann Martin's Apple Paperbacks include *Yours Turly, Shirley*; *Ten Kids, No Pets*; *With You and Without You*; *Bummer Summer*; and all the other books in the Baby-sitters Club series.

THE BABY-SITTERS CLUB

Look for BSC #79

MARY ANNE BREAKS THE RULES

We were all gabbing away when the front door opened.

"Hello! I'm ba-ack!" Mrs. Kuhn sang out. Her keys jingled as she walked toward the kitchen. "Guess who didn't have to wait at the doc — "

She never finished her sentence. She just stopped in the kitchen doorway.

Her eyes flickered from Logan to me. Her smile tightened.

In that moment I realized I had never told her about Logan. Never asked if he could come over, either.

I hadn't thought it was a big deal. Mrs. Kuhn probably wouldn't have, either, except for two small facts.

Logan was a boy. I was a girl.

And I looked like the world's biggest sneak.

"Hi, Mommy!" Patsy screamed, running to hug Mrs. Kuhn's knees.

"Hello, sweetheart." Mrs. Kuhn gave her daughter a hug, but her eyes never left mine. "So we have a . . . visitor?"

Logan stood up with a smile. "Hello, Mrs. Kuhn. I'm Logan Bruno."

"What a surprise," Mrs. Kuhn said.

"He's the *best* athlete," Jake insisted.

"Ha ha." Logan's laugh sounded so forced. I could tell Mrs. Kuhn was making him nervous. "Jake's getting pretty good himself."

"Now, Mary Anne," Mrs. Kuhn barged on, "correct me if I'm wrong, but I don't believe we discussed anyone else coming over today."

"I'm okay, Mom," Jake chimed in. "Logan's been here before."

"*Has* he?" she asked.

"Sure. He's Mary Anne's boyfriend."

Ugh.

I felt as if someone had pulled a drawstring around my stomach.

Read all the books about Claudia in

THE BABY-SITTERS CLUB

by Ann M. Martin

by Ann M. Martin

More titles... ▶

The Baby-sitters Club titles continued...

Available wherever you buy books...or use this order form.

Scholastic Inc., P.O. Box 7502, 2931 E. McCarty Street, Jefferson City, MO 65102

Please send me the books I have checked above. I am enclosing $_____
(please add $2.00 to cover shipping and handling). Send check or money order - no
cash or C.O.D.s please.

Name _____ Birthdate_____

Address _____

City_____ State/Zip _____

Please allow four to six weeks for delivery. Offer good in the U.S. only. Sorry, mail orders are not
available to residents of Canada. Prices subject to change.

THE BIGGEST BSC SWEEPSTAKES EVER!

Scholastic and Ann M. Martin want to thank all of the Baby-sitters Club fans for a cool 100 million books in print! Celebrate by sending in your entry now!

ENTER AND YOU CAN WIN:

• *10 Grand Prizes:* Win one of ten $2,500 prizes! Your cash prize is good towards any artistic, academic, or sports pursuit. Take a dance workshop, go to soccer camp, get a violin tutor, learn a foreign language! You decide and Scholastic will pay the expense up to $2,500 value. Sponsored by Scholastic Inc., the Ann M. Martin Foundation, Kid Vision, Milton Bradley® and Kenner® Products.

• *100 First Prizes:* Win one of 100 fabulous runner-up gifts selected for you by Scholastic including a limited supply of BSC videos, autographed limited editions of Ann Martin's upcoming holiday book, T-shirts, board games and other fabulous merchandise!

Just fill in the coupon below or write the information on a 3" x 5" piece of paper and mail to: **THE BSC REMEMBERS SWEEPSTAKES,** Scholastic Inc., P.O. Box 7500, 2931 East McCarty Street, Jefferson City, MO 65102. Entries must be postmarked by10/31/94.

Send to Scholastic Inc., P.O. Box 7500, 2931 East McCarty Street, Jefferson City, MO 65102.

THE BSC REMEMBERS SWEEPSTAKES

Name _____ Birthdate _____

Address _____ Phone# _____

City _____ State _____ Zip _____

Where did you buy this book?   ❏ Bookstore   ❏ Other(Specify)

Name of Bookstore _____

BSCR

ENTER SCHOLASTIC'S

THE BSC REMEMBERS
SWEEPSTAKES

Official Rules:

No purchase necessary. To enter use the official entry form or a 3" x 5" piece of paper and hand print your full name, complete address, day telephone number and birthdate. Enter as often as you wish, one entry to an envelope. Mechanically reproduced entries are void. Mail to THE BSC REMEMBERS Sweepstakes at the address provided on the previous page, postmarked by 10/31/94. Scholastic Inc. is not responsible for late, lost or postage due mail. Sweepstakes open to residents of the U.S.A. 6-15 years old upon entering. Employees of Scholastic Inc., Kid Vision, Milton Bradley Inc., Kenner Inc., Ann M. Martin Foundation, their affiliates, subsidiaries, dealers, distributors, printers, mailers, and their immediate families are ineligible. Prize winners will be randomly drawn from all eligible entries under the supervision of Smiley Promotion Inc., an independent judging organization whose decisions are final. Prizes: Ten Grand Prizes each $2,500 awarded toward any artistic, academic or sports pursuit approved by Scholastic Inc. Winner may also choose $2,500 cash payment. An approved pursuit costing less than $2,500 must be verified by bona fide invoice and presented to Scholastic Inc. prior to 7/31/95 to receive the cash difference. One hundred First Prizes each a selection by Scholastic Inc. of BSC videos, Ann Martin books, t-shirts and games. Estimated value each $10.00. Sweepstakes void where prohibited, subject to all federal, state, provincial, local laws and regulations. Odds of winning depend on the number of entries received. Prize winners are notified by mail. Grand Prize winners and parent/legal guardian are mailed a Affidavit of Eligibility/ Liability/ Publicity/Release to be executed and returned within 14 days of its date or an alternate winner may be drawn. Only one prize allowed a person or household. Taxes on prize, expenses incurred outside of prize provision and any injury, loss or damages incurred by acceptance and use of prizes are the sole responsibility of the winners and their parent/legal guardian. Prizes cannot be exchanged, transferred or cashed. Scholastic Inc. reserves the right to substitute prizes of like value if any offered are unavailable and to use the names and likenesses of prize winners without further compensation for advertising and promotional use. Prizes that are unclaimed or undelivered to winner's address remain the property of Scholastic Inc. For a Winners List, please send a stamped, addressed envelope to THE BSC REMEMBERS Sweepstakes Winners, Smiley Promotion Inc., 271 Madison Avenue, #802, New York, N.Y. 10016 after 11/30/94. Residents of Washington state may omit return stamp.

Celebrate the Holiday with

THE BABY-SITTERS CLUB®

Secret Santa
by Ann M. Martin

It's Christmastime, and the Baby-sitters are
holding a Secret Santa drawing.
Each Club member puts one wish in a hat,
and then draws someone else's wish to
grant. You'll have to open their mail to
discover how this special holiday turns
out — and how the BSC members make one
little girl's Christmas the best ever!

**Real
cards, letters,
and friendship
necklaces
for you
and a
friend!**

If you loved *The Baby-sitters Club Chain Letter*,
you'll love this perfect holiday gift for all BSC fans!

Coming in October to a bookstore near you.

BSCSS294

Don't miss out on
The All New

THE BABY-SITTERS CLUB®

Claudia • Kristy • Mallory • Stacey • Dawn • Mary Anne • Jessi

**Wow! It's really them-
the new Baby-sitters Club dolls!**

Your favorite Baby-sitters Club characters have come to life in these
beautiful collector dolls. Each doll wears her own unique clothes and jewelry.
They look just like the girls you have imagined! The dolls also come with their own
individual stories in special edition booklets that you'll find nowhere else.

**Look for the new Baby-sitters Club collection...
coming soon to a store near you!** **Kenner®**

Create Your Own Mystery Stories!

MYSTERY GAME!

WHO: Boyfriend   **WHY:** Romance

WHAT: Phone Call   **WHERE:** Dance

Use the special Mystery Case card to pick WHO did it, WHAT was involved, WHY it happened and WHERE it happened. Then dial secret words on your Mystery Wheels to add to the story! Travel around the special Stoneybrook map gameboard to uncover your friends' secret word clues! Finish four baby-sitting jobs and find out all the words to win. Then have everyone join in to tell the story!